IF MY FATHER DIES I GIVE BIRTH TO HIM AGAIN

SELECTED WRITINGS OF KOLA BOOF

If My Father Dies I Give Birth to Him Again

ISBN: 978-0-578-02896-5

The editor acknowledges the following kind permissions to reproduce the works of Kola Boof:

Nile River Woman

Reprinted by permission of Door of Kush/Atlantic Library

Diary of a Lost Girl

Reprinted by permission of Door of Kush/Atlantic Library

Long Train to the Redeeming Sin: Stories of African Women

Reprinted by permission of Door of Kush/Atlantic Library

Flesh and the Devil

Reprinted by permission of Door of Kush/Atlantic Library

Published by

VALLEY PRESS

PO Box 1691

Rutherford, NJ 07070

Mark Fogarty: Editor and Publisher

Tony Fradkin: Cover art

Table of Contents

IF MY FATHER DIES I GIVE BIRTH TO HIM AGAIN

Selected Writings of Kola Boof

Kola Boof is an extravagantly talented writer—and it's time she gets her due for being a gifted and accomplished author of poetry, fiction and memoir. So I've undertaken to pick some of her best writing and showcase it both as an introduction to her work for those who don't know it yet, and as a well-deserved reminder for those who do.

I first became aware of Kola in 2002, after a major US newspaper took a wrongheaded swipe at her in print. I was soon to discover that Kola was a lightning rod for controversy with a major talent for pissing people off. But that side of her never interested me all that much. I discovered, via her website (www.kolaboof.com), that Kola was a gifted poet. I also read for the first time, through her, about the horrible things that were happening in Kola's birthplace, the Sudan. I had never read the word *Darfur* before. Kola Boof was an important early voice in America alerting us to the unbelievably bad things going on there.

Next I read her powerful, gutsy book of short stories, *Long Train to the Redeeming Sin: Stories of African Women* (also known as *The Goddess Flower* overseas*)*. This book kicked at me hard. Rough around the edges, it nevertheless has a tremendous cumulative punch. Kola's stories of African women tend to tell of short, bloody lives, full of violence, rape, intolerance and injustice. And a very big heart beats behind the book, the heart of an author who has both a barely contained fury over what is being done to her heroines, and a barely contained sorrow over their devastations. Anger and empathy drive these stories of broken and forsaken everyday goddesses into a very high gear. And you can see the seeds of a major literary artist being sown in these angry and mournful pages.

My hunch that Kola also is a talented and visionary poet was confirmed when I read her book of poetry, *Nile River Woman* (which revises and extends her first book of poems, *Every Little Bit Hurts*). These poems are deeply beautiful, dipped in the same Nilotic blend of compassion and sorrow that allows her to achieve a terrible clarity, purposefulness, empathy, and wisdom for the women, past and present, who have that mighty river at the center of their existences.

After reading these two books I was interested in knowing more about this Sudanese-American author (she also has Egyptian and Somali heritage). From correspondence with her, an eyeful of the amazing and seemingly neverending turbulent publicity about her in the media, and an early copy of her memoirs, *Diary of a Lost Girl*, I was able to piece together an amazing story.

Kola was born Naima bint Harith, the daughter of an Arab father and a black Sudanese woman. She was born in either 1969 or 1972 depending on whether you believe her aunt (the earlier date) or the Sudanese government (the later), in Omdurman, which is on the Nile River near Khartoum, the Sudanese capital.

Kola's Nilotic years ended in a hurry, though, with the government-ordered killing of her parents, within her earshot, when she was seven or eight years old. Spurned by her Arab grandmother for being too dark, Kola was adopted out of Sudan by an aid agency. She was one of the first of the lost girls and lost boys of Sudan who would find their way to America, some enduring Biblical plagues of murder, rape, starvation and animal predation on their perilous way.

Kola was adopted into an African American family living in the funky Anacostia Park section of Washington, DC. Her adoptive family was big and loving but could not wholly make up for the trauma she had endured and the culture shock of landing in a new country where she didn't speak the native language. She learned English by watching soap operas, and got her first taste of her later vocation by reading *The Bluest Eye* by Toni Morrison. Kola grew into an alienated teenage runaway with little direction but lots of energy, a lost girl strung between two painful heritages.

As a young woman, Kola returned to Africa to try to make sense of that part of her divided heritage. She lived an adventurous and exotic lifestyle, acting in African low budget movies and making the scene as a party girl for some of the most prominent leaders of African countries. Along the way she had affairs with people who would become well-known in America years later, terrorists including the most notorious of them all, Osama bin Laden (well before 2001, of which she had no knowledge, it should be noted).

And sometime along the way, back in Africa, the lost and traumatized girl Naima morphed into a potent and fearless writer, ready to fight for the right of her lost and damaged African women to be heard. She also wanted to call attention to the situation festering into the hellhole we now know the Sudan is, with its black peoples suffering genocidal oppression by the Islamist government in Khartoum. And the name she took reflected both sides of her. It reflected her African heritage, from the kola nuts African kids eat as snacks and the ebullient *boof*! sound of African drums. At the same time it also reflected her American side, through its near matches with Coca Cola and

Betty Boop, an early cartoon flapper. Kola Boof was born, and the new writer released two novels (in Arabic) and a book of poetry, *Every Little Bit Hurts*. This was followed by *The Goddess Flower*, the first iteration of *Long Train*.

These early works and the eventual revelation of the bin Laden affair created a firestorm for Kola, including threats on her life, and she returned to the United States, where she has lived in semi-seclusion ever since. One casualty of all the high-decibel chatter about her Page Six-style celebrity has been her literary career. People have been reading about Kola Boof, and that has gotten in the way of more people actually reading her. That's why I have decided to cut through all the chatter and present Kola here without reference (insofar as that's possible) to her high-octane public life.

Reading her novel *Flesh and the Devil* just underscored for me what a terrific writer Kola is. The book was written in Arabic, in Africa (she also has an African novel not published in America with the provocative title *Pure Nigger Evil*). It shows her at her mythopoetic best, especially in the beginning, where she throws off myths and African creation stories with zest and world-making abandon.

Kola in the media can be harsh and strident, taking no prisoners and taking lots of flak in return. But that's only part of her personality. The first time I met her, at a restaurant inside one of California's old mission churches, I was impressed by her powerful stature (she is over six feet tall) and regal bearing. She was gentle and charming but I also got a flash of shyness, something of the reticence the young Naima bint Harith must have felt to be newly transplanted to a strange new country.

The second time I met her (and there have been only two times), I introduced her at a reading she gave at the Schomburg Center in Harlem. Here I was impressed by the seriousness she brings to her vocation. Kola gave a three-hour performance. She read, sang, danced, told stories, answered questions, signed books and threw herself into the reading with focus and style.

Afterwards, as we were walking to the car, she stumbled into me several times and I realized that she had given all of her energy to the event. She was totally exhausted.

2.

If My Father Dies I Give Birth to Him Again represents my selection of Kola's best writing to date. What I have selected for this volume is examples of Kola Boof's best literary work, rather than her writing on race and politics, which we have agreed to disagree on. What you'll see presented here is outstanding work from a major literary talent just now entered into her most productive years.

From *Nile River Woman* I have chosen a dozen of her best poems. They are written out of crystal clarity about the plight of Kola's Nilotic women, past and present. It occurs to me that these poems also function as prayers, offered up to God or the gods of the native religions, for aid and succor, for acknowledgement, for protection. These women are sacred to Kola, goddess flowers, and they have been brutalized and defiled. The poems also show the grounding and the strength that Kola has derived from her African traditions, the strengths she shows in being a battling woman warrior for those she loves and values. And the poems also show Kola's bedrock womanism, in her deep belief in the power and glory there is to being a woman.

From *Long Train to the Redeeming Sin* I have chosen two of her best stories: "Boy Magic (a Love Story)," and "Day of Vow." "Boy Magic" is the tale of an outrage, a young African woman raped by a wealthy landowner. Traveling to the capital city to obtain justice, she is instead thrown into jail for libeling her attacker. Meantime, she has contracted AIDs (known in Africa as "the woman's disease") and faces the prospect of dying in jail. She is saved from this by a white aid worker. A more rigid writer would have Nuntandi's AIDs come from her rapist, but in fact Nuntandi has contracted the disease from her consensual lover, with whom she enjoys a blissful liaison.

Kola's story is both outraged over Nuntandi's bleak fate and overjoyed at her exercise of her natural rights. This is a bracing morality tale, which swerves and swoops over a wide emotional terrain and underlines the hard-earned dignity of this dying African girl.

"Day of Vow" is a powerful fable of an African girl with a tremendous talent for glassblowing that is co-opted by her white employer. As with Nuntandi's story, there is both a wretched debasement and a thrilling empowerment of the wondrous gift she has been born with. Finally, she is raped by her employer's son, an act which sets off a violent aftermath that ends the story, and the book, with a bang. This is a story about creativity and the immense power it can bring, along with dire consequences inevitable in a racist society (South Africa).

From *Diary of a Lost Girl* I have chosen not the familiar and incendiary account of her time with bin Laden, but Kola's brilliant, razor-sharp account of her short time in Africa, growing up along her nurturing Nile, before the awful murder of her parents. This is a tour de force of memory and reconstruction from her African family, of her Arab archaeologist father Harith, and her jet-black mother Jiddi, a woman of amazingly few words, and the improbable "blue sky" love between them that produced her. It is a story of sharp-tongued Auntie Ramah, and the women who gather at the mighty river, and the ritual infibulation the girls have to endure, and the anti-slavery opinions that put her father on the government's bad side. Related with the visionary clarity of a dream, it remembers her mother's great beauty and the sights and smells and foods of her Sudanese childhood. It is a brilliantly detailed happy time that ends in disaster with the murder of her parents in the courtyard of Kola's home. A horrific night with their dead bodies is followed by an awful repudiation of her by her Arab grandmother. With its surefooted juxtapositions of great happiness and sudden devastation, it is a beautiful piece of writing by a true Bint il Nil (daughter of the Nile).

From *Flesh and the Devil* I have chosen the gorgeously mythic beginning section. It is doubly impressive because it describes or creates myths for West African tribes that lived far from the East African people Kola came from. Her mythmaking is grand and totally delightful, such as "The sky was the man... and the sea was the woman... and they hated each other!" The rain which they use as an agent to meet, the angry moon that curses women and causes them to bleed, the very passionate connections made between the first men and women, all of this is painted on a wide and bright canvass and is a joy to read. Later, things will grow grimmer with the advent of white slavers and the forced diaspora to American slavery and the doings of modern-day African Americans, but in the beginning this is the freshest and most imaginative of all possible worlds.

What's next for this talented writer? Kola has three books upcoming: a book of poetic identity called *Egyptian Sudanese American*, and novels with the irresistible titles *The Sexy Part of the Bible* and *Virgins in the Beehive*. I suspect she has a popular success ahead of her, as the drumbeats around her die down and America learns to pay attention to her superior writing skills. Entranced by the daytime dramas she learned English from as a girl, and the silent movies she absorbed (and which she often uses to name her books), it would be unlikely that these specifically American artforms wouldn't find their way into her work (as they already have in the second part of *Flesh and the Devil*). These popular rhythms inform her style just as much as her more obvious African American models, like Alice Walker and Toni Morrison. That's a potent mix, and the world would do well to be ready for it.

What is the essence of Kola Boof's talent and appeal? Kola's best work clearly announces the great thing that it is to be a woman (to paraphrase Whitman), and the unimaginable travesties that have been committed against women throughout the ages. And for this she has begun to get her proper notice, as with the Woman to Woman Pen Award she recently received from a Swedish feminist group. I predict there will be more awards coming. Her work is also poignantly on target about the long, hard road of getting your soul in order. Kola has had a longer and harder road than most of the rest of us, and her story, and her stories, are a triumph.

The title I give this selection of Kola's work comes from *Flesh and the Devil.* In fact it is the theme of this story of 26,000 years of reincarnated Africans and African Americans living and dying and living again, through African conflicts, slaveholder depredations and modern African American lives: *If my father dies, I give birth to him again.* True in her real life with her own two sons, it is also the central theme of her best work. This idea connects the shattered young girl with the dead parents to the powerful artist who brings them unforgettably back to life again. It is the power of witness and endurance, the temporary triumph that will have to do until the girls of Sudan are lost no more, the women of Africa are freed from AIDs, rape and violence, and African Americans continue the glacially slow (but real) progress toward full equality. The power of giving birth and nurturing the next generation will always be manifest in everything Kola Boof writes, and it connects her to the many generations of her foremothers, back to the one who is the foremother of us all.

–MARK FOGARTY

If My Father Dies I Give Birth to Him Again

From

Nile River Woman

A RIVER TO BLEED IN

Once a month, we know that God is with us.
She is the red dragon
flowing from our lips like the Nile.
At the bottom of the river we abide her.
Our feet planted in the mud…mud that is
softer, finer than our inside mouth.

We are the daughters of the Nile.
We are women, Yes.
We have two mouths to speak with.

We are the daughters of *buk,* the children of the
Sun. We are His lasting vine…jism sprung.
So that there is heart and mind to paint the soul.
So that once we bleed no more, we are the Goddess
…wisdom's beauty Old.
Divine and bloody goddess.

nipple of life…ancient and tomorrows

Ma-Mah

ROUND YOUNG VIRGIN

I remember when the ocean
first started

A shell-pod (a baby) washed in with the first
tide

(and that was our music then)

Orange sand turning lavender *monthlies* into purple
blood produced an orange moon
(and we thought we could take it down and eat it!)

black pearl
black pearl

(we rolled you under our tongues)

Everything
was so fresh, precise and perfect,
because we were not long for this world.
Not yet laughing...because we had to
first

get bored with crying.
Tima

EVERY LITTLE BIT HURTS

In broad daylight
I am expected to see nothing.
I am a girl; low and dark
as the crease of shadow from
which I swam.
I have no hair like
the Arab woman (whose hair
is like silk and smells
like snot)—and when the
White woman comes to my face
(ME/the Black man's mother)—I
think of the penis.

The men want us to hate one
another. It makes them
feel safe…to have the White (day)
and the Black (night) denying the
flowsongs of blood—the River.

every little bit hurts, God.

In Africa, we have no cold oceans/We accept
that you made us from fire.
We sing to the lioness

and pray for when the hate will go away
in broad daylight
(from where it came)

O God, darkest father!
We are Black Men's daughters;
wet, tired and hungry.
At our heels the demon snaps
mightily no matter
what beam of wind we direct; what
beam of sun we deflect.

For out of bare breasts
our hearts are LEAPING
of warm oceans; the brown eyes
of our daughters
staring into the stretchmark of
a blue body's sorrow.

We kiss it up to God. Because every
little bit hurts.

THE WIDOW's BLOOD

Illuminate me, waterfall
I have swallowed a moon. I am
stone (that smooth)
Sheaths of tears, curtains of sea
I am
where my soul enters me.

Illuminate me, death

Beneath Horeessa, I planted his head.
In my mouth I keep his tooth. In my mind, I
ovalize his square jaw to clay
I have been a fire-lit cave in which he hid out
all night (as men do)

Illuminate me, sunlight
Make me fine like sand
Make my dying blood patient
for a time
for a time

CHRISTMAS ON THE NILE

(a poem about Kola's birth mother)

She is mighty-mighty
(and I remember her)

I remember her toes
piercing the bloody Nile; the
glimpse of leg
beneath wool

I remember her blackness
--so sheer and deep like the
slippery hue of a charcoal panther

beauty abstract and beguiling.

I remember the roundness of her
face,
the diamonds in her eyes...and the
merriment of a hair like
wool: salt-jagged and knotty.

On Jesus birthday; I remember
The Holy/unforgettable

BINT IL NIL

I want a new religion.
The one our mothers had in the river.

I am tired of Jesus and Mohammed.
I am tired of man's foot.
I am tired of White man's mother.
I am weary...from doing nothing about it.

I want my own religion.
I want my real mother.

Africa, I want you.

Make me pregnant with God.
Our own perfect babies...black as perfection.
Tall as the sky. Healthy as light sparkling on
Clear water.

I want my own religion.
I want my own voice.
I want my own face.
I want my own hair.
I am Naima / the one who is victorious
the one
who is praying

BLACK BEAUTY's TOTEM
I wish to find the swell
of constant waters

...and the death of the locust night

I wish to find the anguished heart
of the blue blackened earthquake
and lay my monkish head against his
armoured chest.

To bless him with full, swollen lips
And behold his darkened portholes
Drinking my softened flesh...oh, but yes

I wish to die as spirits then...

droplets

lost and swishing forever
deep within my purple folds
sweet

like birth and no regret

NILE RIVER WOMAN

(a Dinka slave of the Sudan)

my feet were bound by eel-skin and river
stones.
my nose and throat were so caked with blood,
I could hardly breathe.
the sun beat my face.
Nothing but hate was in my heart.

You came into the world anyway.

I split open and you came.
For that time, I had to stop running.
In the trees near an artery
--of blue shallow water,
I had to learn your heartbeat and breathe
inside of you and make human sound.
Against my fur-hole I warmed you
and from my breasts I fed you.

I didn't mind after a while that you had come,
But I thought about killing you.

I thought about clearing a path—to run.

DOLPHIN (DURING PREGNANCY)

On morning's fin
I gave birth to a new manchild
Into the water—out to the sun
I am naked because I have done nothing wrong.
I am a woman (Yes)
I have two mouths to speak with.

Between disagreements eternal
Blood of fat men where they burst from life
Sudan and crocodiles / Sun and blackness
Undoing the death

I am revolution's woman
on morning's fin
Penetrating the surface—diving into the womb
Where my son is feasting
Where I dreamt of gallant daughters; dark as the
blood in eggs...yellow as straw and sudd; caroling
after my mothering
Black stick fingers scratching at my scalp, parting
the knotted ancient proof (my natural mate)

Where the sun catches my wet tail
and our dreams take to feasting
before we fast *(inside me)*

THERE IS SLAVERY IN SUDAN

The lonely war imprisons even the sun.
Licking at the scrotum of an ungodly Imam.
Charcoal children chained to the back doors of
Arab households.
Charcoal children fed like prison stock
From doggy bowls.

The lonely war bestills all Gods.

But I am the future. I am love.

I am that future of my open scalp's freedom.
Traveling.

I fear not Satan
nor his brothers, nor his religion.
Selling Sudan.
Dinka girl…raped and sold for fourteen dollars.
Nuer fathers gunned down near the marketplace.
Shilluk mothers, tongues removed, sent to Palestine.
To be slaves.

Lost boys…living it up in the Pet cream of America.

NUNTANDI

trickle slowly wet; Oh cry
like the unobtainable butterfly in the
garden's wilting goodbye

Where my parents are buried again

I am not naked because of sin, but
because
I am brown and red and black all inside
Where the beauty I reached for made
poison

I am trapped in the belly of the teardrop

I am related to blood (Positive)
I feel like slime inside the snail
I am related

I am your floor inside the jail

Singing
trickle slowly wet; Oh cry

please…Oh please
love me, too, God

THANKSGIVING DAY

I make no sound, but a heartbeat

I take no liberties with the devil
nor do I
smoke his dandruff
or cut his pathways
because
life is much too hard

and I love the slow pace of my God
and the cornered grins of
my ghosts—I love the act of will
I savor the days of the earth
I love the height of the sky

I cherish every black man
With an unheard sorrow
because
our graves are just the same

and I live for the echo of my children;
listening for the bolt
with the silent faith
with the silent faith
that they have in me.
I make no sound…but a heartbeat.

From

DIARY OF A LOST GIRL

BINT IL NIL

My creation began as the result of an arranged "*blue sky love*" between two extraordinary people, neither of whom were from Sudan, but both of whom found themselves settled there, circa 1961, in a love nest right on the banks of Omdurman's Nile River.

Mahdi Pappuh (*my father, my God*), Harith Bin Farouk was an extremely tall, butterscotch-colored White Arab Egyptian with coily "mixed" hair--more nappy like Hebrew hair than slick like an Arab's hair. He was an archeologist and was studying religious coffees in Somalia when he first laid eyes on my mother (Mommysweet), whom he told me he fell in love with the very tender moment he first saw her. She was a fourteen year old charcoal-colored Gisi-Waaq Oromo girl--Gisi (her family name), Waaq (her lineage, The Crow), Oromo (her tribe, Nomadic coffee worshippers). Her name was Jiddi and her father was her tribe's Chief, which is why she was called Princess Jiddi.

In our world, men pay a dowry to the girl's father for marriage rights, and in Sudan (where Pappuh owned a large house), the Northern men generally have only one wife.

Pappuh Mahdi immediately attempted to purchase Mommysweet for marriage, but because her father was the Chief and because they considered Pappuh a "*white man*" (as non-black Arabs are categorized as *white* in Africa), the dowry price was extremely high...and the most Pappuh was able to do was deposit a down payment. He told me that it took him until Mommysweet was seventeen to pay it off (in cattle), but that it was well worth it. Pappuh married her twice—first in a ceremony with her clanspeople and then at his family's mosque in Egypt. He was thirty-five to her seventeen, which is normally considered an ideal match, but the fact that she was so incredibly dark skinned--what we call "*Biblical Days Black*" (charcoal people, the originals)--didn't sit well with Pappuh's White identified Egyptian family. And please note, that although there have recently been colleagues of my father's in London who claim that he was Kushaf (a type of mixed race Nubian-Turkish tribe who live in North Egypt), that is not true--my father was Arab Egyptian, yes with Turkish blood, but no immediate Nubian blood. Regardless that these men in London worked with and knew my father, they are mistaken about his ethnicity.

Pappuh's family, the Kolbookeks, had spent decades trying to breed any signs of Africa out of their bloodline. My grandmother, Najet, in fact, never forgave Pappuh for bringing the *root* back into the family tree. She cursed him and complained bitterly about his lifelong obsession with the "Hemetic blood" (the blood of the original authentic ancient Egyptians), which was now considered a defect of the Cushite, Ethiopian, Somali, Nuba and Nubian peoples--as well as the dark Egyptian ghetto people of the Upper Nile (Southern Egypt is called "The Upper Nile," with many blacks living in the Kom Ombo region)--but this blood is "*not a stain,*" you understand, when it's in the veins of the Beja and Arab ruling class in Egypt (of which our family was still not accepted by, because of grandmother Najet's own great grandmother--a pureblooded Falasha--*a Black Jew*).

Najet would weep openly and complain about Mahdi Pappuh's tenure at the University in France years earlier where all he ever wrote about was his fascination with the "*abeed*" (Arab word for "slave stock" but used as "*nigger*") and their grand history in Egypt. He had not returned home with a lovely, blond French wife--but instead with a high yellow, big-lipped nappyheaded Black American girl from Georgetown, D.C. (1956). Grandmother Najet had nearly had a heart attack! (to Egyptians before the civil rights movement, Black Americans were considered to be "*the lowest of all niggerstock*")--and when he married Princess Jiddi in 1961, Grandmother Najet all but disowned him. She commanded him, "Leave Egypt and take Sheba with you! What will my friends think of me with mud on my foot!?"

And not only Grandmother Najet, but the entire family worried tremendously about the way they (as a clan) would be perceived by having a charcoal black wife in the stead. It was too radical.

So, you see, this was why my birth parents settled in Sudan instead of Egypt. Mahdi Pappuh wanted very desperately to be considered "a black man," and in fact, he spent his entire life depressed about it, to the point of becoming a heroin addict, because of course, in Africa--you have to be *black* to be black, and even more importantly, you have to possess the Crown (the nappy African hair) to truly be an African and a black person. There is no one drop rule--anywhere on the continent. You're either black or you're half-caste (mulatto) or Berber-Beja (mixed race). Arab is white. Black Arabs (like me) are "abeed" (niggers). It is not how Black Americans claim ("*Africans come in many colors*")--that is not how we live in Africa; there are terrible caste systems, and most mulattos and mixed people would rather die than be called black or be grouped with blacks. The Dinkas, Nubians, Nuers, Shilluks, Lothu, Oromo, Masai, all of whom befriended and studied by my father, all of whom greatly respected and loved my father, all of whom accepted him as one of their tribe--would never--accept him as a "*black man.*" To his face, they told him: "you de white man, be proud." And this used to kill him inside. He often told me that this was why he married charcoal Mommysweet. He said that it was his life's dream to have black sons.

Unfortunately, Mommysweet gave birth to six boys in a row--all born dead with their umbilical cords wrapped around their necks. I was her seventh pregnancy (and it's my understanding that I'm not the only seventh born-first girl after six stillborn sons in the literary world--the American author Gayl Jones, I've been told, is also the seventh born first girl in her family--so yes, it obviously does happen, and I refuse to believe that it's witchcraft). My Auntie Ramah (Mommysweet's best friend and dressmaker) told me that when I was born (which took place around noontime right on the banks of the Nile as Mommysweet was washing clothes) and they washed off and presented me to Pappuh, announcing that I was a healthy baby girl, he took one look at me and cried out, indignantly, "*Bitch*!"

Auntie Ramah and I would get such a bellylaugh whenever she told me this story because it was the way that Auntie Ramah could tell a thing. She was one of those plump, down-by-the-riverside African women who can take anything hurting inside a person and transform it into ferris wheels of laughter. Metaphor was her gift.

Anyway, after I was born, Mommysweet never became pregnant again. It was amazing. People all over Omdurman declared her to be a jinn (a powerfully evil spirit) and avoided her whenever possible. They declared Pappuh a wimp for not killing her (as <u>some</u> Muslim men are known to do in our world if a wife bore no sons), and they truly believed--with good reason--that Mommysweet was a *mute*. In fact, Mommysweet made sure that people thought she was a mute. I can honestly say that in my entire seven years as her daughter, I think she only spoke (using her mouth) maybe eight or nine times tops.

This is not an exaggeration. Only Auntie Ramah could speak Mommysweet's Oromo language (Ramah being a red skinned Oromo from a clan in Tanzania that had bright orange-brown complexions), and although Pappuh had taught Mommysweet how to speak flawless Arabic, her religion of silence hurt me very deeply growing up. I was, after all, the only child in Omdurman whose mother never spoke to her.

She would come to the doorway of my bedroom every morning, just before the sun came up, and stand there with a basin of water until I woke up. Her presence, of course, woke me. Then she would smile and come to bed, roughly washing my face and hands with a hot rag, which was followed by brushing my teeth and having me spit and chew guddaim rinds. After that, she would give my hair 150 brushstrokes exactly--all the while studying my facial features intently, as though her stare could magically transform them. I looked more like my father and I think she had been waiting for me to look more like her, but sadly, I never did inherit Mommysweet's beauty, and yet I was just as spellbound by it as Pappuh and the men in town were.

I remember her face to be the black perfection of moon-lit nightwater on an African lake. Her body was firm but waif-looking, very thin as most East African women are thin, with a long swan's neck and delicate little hands and feet (which I did inherit). Her hair swung down her back like thick flowing robes of rough, knotted dark foliage and her nose was more slender and "upper class" than Pappuh's bulbous Arab one. She had full lips and high cheekbones, a large forehead (which I also inherited) and knife-like eyes, black and shiny as a Crow (Mommysweet and Ramah's tribes both worshipped the Crow as their God). She moved about the streets of Omdurman like an *S*-shaped cobra defiantly floating over lava coals--always with a basket atop her head, always dressed in flowing white. The Nubian women would call her "Baby Sister" to her face, but behind her back they would make fun of her name, Jiddi, because it means "*bearer of sons.*"

After washing me up and brushing out my nappy, shoulder-length hair, Mommysweet would kiss me three times--once on the forehead and once over both eyes, very gently and with a linger. Then I would be draped in one of the white cotton dresses she made for me by hand and a burka placed over my hair. Pappuh would usually be waiting downstairs for me, so as to share the first of his five prayers for the day (which is not normal).

In our culture, the men are served their meals first, before women and children, and must eat separately from the women and children. Boys, once about twelve, can start eating with men...but in our home, there were no boys, no live-in uncles, so Mahdi Pappuh broke the rules and had me eat all my meals with him. He taught me to keep this a secret and to never speak of it outside our home, because the mosque could have him imprisoned or even stoned to death for such a transgression.

Mommysweet would let me help her prepare the meals (to learn cooking, of course) and breakfast time, because of Pappuh being home in the mornings and telling us jokes from the newspaper, became my favorite time of day. Mommysweet would fix Pappuh's breakfast of Aseeda (a sweet porridge like cream of wheat) with panfried perch or tiger fish crumbled up in it, and with that she would serve him a stack of Kisra with honey poured over it (Kisra is a flat bread made from corn that everyone in Sudan eats every day, several times a day). To wash it all down, Pappuh would have a tall glass of fruit juice--usually tabaldi juice, orange juice or aradaib juice.

Mommysweet and I would have Jbna (coffee), but we'd make it Oromo style--*fried* first--and then add hot water and ginger to the caramel from the beans and pour it into tiny porcelain cups with two lumps of sugar, and occasionally, a little goat's milk.

For our breakfast, we'd have the same Aseeda porridge, but with a side of crunchy deep fried locusts (which tastes like a combination of shrimp and french fries)...and then Pappuh would be reading his newspaper, and all of a sudden, he'd look up as though startled and proclaim, "*Why Naima*!...they've written about you in the newspaper this morning!"

And each morning I would look to Mommysweet with a panicked expression of shock on my face, wondering what the story of the day would be, and Mommysweet would give a hearty giggle (but never say a word), and then Mahdi Pappuh would go on to read some silly imaginary story, "Why it says right here...blah, blah, blah."

In our mosque..."music" was considered evil. It wasn't allowed. But every morning, Pappuh would take Mommysweet's hand and sing to her after breakfast. He would grab her and kiss her and make her laugh. He would sing: "*O...blue sky love.*"

And those were days of heaven for me, my little life...before the evil angels descended upon Sudan. Or rather--before I was old enough to recognize that even in blue skies, they do flutter about.

~~

Pappuh Mahdi began to shoot heroin when I was around six years old. I'm taking my Egyptian Uncle Kar's word that that's when it began, anyway--and I think he's right. I honestly did not know about it in the sense that he was "*on drugs.*" Of course, no one explained anything to me and I had just assumed that he was suffering from some Muslim men's disease (they had so many mysteries to them) that couldn't be discussed with females and was being treated for it. In retrospect, now that I've grown up and seen much of the world, I can recall that he had mild hallucinations and that he did look possessed, as though he wasn't Pappuh Mahdi anymore but rather someone imitating Mahdi Pappuh...and yet because he and Mommysweet would be murdered by the time I was seven...I never did get to really witness the destructive and dramatic effects of heroin abuse. I thank God that I didn't have to watch my father reduced to such a state, although, as I said, evil angels began to flutter about.

In writing this autobiography, I have tried very hard to piece together everything from our lives in Sudan as accurately as I can (with the help of my Uncle Kar and several people), but I still don't have definite command of some of the intricate details of Pappuh's problems with varied officials in Sudan. But I do think (from memory) that our trouble started when the mayor's office wrote a note to Pappuh threatening to take our house away if he didn't shut up about something, but exactly what that first matter was all about, I don't know. Pappuh began to complain that he needed to earn more money to "*finance his opinions.*"

Our home in Omdurman was *very large* and comfortable. Our financial status came in cycles; we would be dirt poor for six months straight and then very wealthy for perhaps an entire year in alternating cycles. Six months poor, one year rich--over and over again. I believe that Mahdi Pappuh was involved in adventures that were not clean, although, I have no idea what they could have been. I only know that he took trips out of the country to "hustle," as he put it, and always returned with lots of money, gold bracelets, fine silks and fresh lion's meat from Ethiopia; chunks of raw diamonds for Mommysweet (she collected diamonds as a hobby). For me, he would bring beautiful pairs of shoes that little Greek and Turkish girls had been privileged enough to throw away. Our home was a happy one and our lives felt secure.

But then, Arab soldiers (white ones) came to our house one afternoon while Pappuh was away on a dig. I myself was at *kwalwa* (school for Muslim girls), but Auntie Ramah told me all about how she and Mommysweet had handled the situation.

The soldiers banged on the kitchen door while Mommysweet and Auntie were snapping peas and shouted that they had been given a "tip" that Mahdi Pappuh owned a collection of devil music (although it's widely spoken in Sudan, Pappuh was the only one in our home who could understand English, and he did indeed own albums by John Coltrane (whose song "Naima" I am named for), Frank Sinatra, Thelonious Monk, Miles Davis, Nina Simone, Aretha Franklin, Dionne Warwick...and his favorite...Mulatu Astatque, the jazz great of Ethiopia). The soldiers insisted that Mommysweet open the kitchen door, but without her husband in the house, she shouted back (as any Sudanese wife would) that she did not have the husband's permission and could not comply with their orders. So naturally, being men and bullies, they kicked in the door and came bursting in--only to find themselves instantly blinded and screaming like women because of the scalding pot of hot Asedi (grits) Mommysweet had thrown in their faces.

By the time they got their wits about them, Auntie Ramah stood before them barefoot with her shirt off so they could see the henna symbols on her loose titties. Muslims on the Nile believe in witches, I promise you that, and when the first one of them could make out her glowing redskinned face and orange nappy hair and the pearl-sparkle in her black raven's eyes--*they knew* who she was. This was "Oromo-Ramah," the most feared fire witch on the Blue Nile. She said: "Khaferi uhn khatiatak" (*pay for your sins, motherfuckers*!). Then she stuck her finger in her pussy hole and fished out a live Sourih-hayyal (a tiny snake that drinks milk from a bowl and is walked on a leash). Of course, to westerners this sounds outlandish, but it's very real—wild women in the countryside who can keep pet snakes in their pussies.

You must understand that there had been a famous incident in our Zarpunni (the governing body of the women's neighborhood) only a year and a half earlier. Auntie Ramah had envoked *rem* (a curse) against a Black American meat vendor. He had become a regular with his cart at the Souq market, but he had the terrible distinction of selling fresh meat to the Noor-byd mdr (White Arab mothers) while selling *rotten meat* to the poor, desperate Black African mothers. His cart was the only one that African mothers could afford in the first place, but at least two little ones had become sick from the meat. It was a very peculiar and mysterious thing for our community to understand, his hate for only Black Africans and *Black* Arabs--not the white ones (of whom there are a great, *great* number in the Sudan, despite what western television shows you), but the situation eventually became so undeniable that two of the mixed-race Beja mothers began donning long, silky Italian wigs thinking this would make a difference, but he still sneered at all African women, refusing to make eye contact, and would offer them only the worst pieces of meat. So one day, Auntie Ramah appeared at his cart and spat a mouthful of goat's milk in his face. That got his attention and everyone else's at the market. She declared that he was actually an evil white woman's spirit inhabiting the body of a black man and that he would be dead in three days.

Three days later...they found him chopped up and packed on ice in his own meat cart.

So now the soldiers were terribly afraid to bother with Auntie Ramah (unless her back was turned--that being the only safe way to kill a witch). She held up the snake and chanted some Oromo words, but the soldiers ran off, she said. And of course, they would not tell their commander that they'd been deterred by two women. No, they would say that they had searched the house and found no devil music. So that it all came out flawless.

But I never will forget coming home that afternoon. Mommysweet, of course, would not *talk* but had fetched me from school early. Auntie Ramah was there when we walked in. She instantly noticed the look on my face and told me not to be afraid and began explaining to me what had happened. She was fully dressed in Muslim garb by then and had one of Pappuh's shirts spread out on the livingroom floor and was "reading" it (the sweat stains, neck dirt) like others might read a palm or look into a crystal ball. I had very little faith, actually, in Auntie's powers, because her own beloved husband, a blue black Mandari, had been kicked to death by Palestinians, because he had been promoted to a coveted post as foreman at a British company in Port Sudan. Ramah's magic had not saved him from the special racism and colorism that the ruling Arab groups (such as Palestinians) reserve for Sudan's nilotic and southern black Africans, so I asked her, "Does that work? What do you see?"

"I see that it's not music that frightens the city officials about your Pappuh." She had soaked his shirt in saved rainwater and was configuring pieces of gum arabic, eucalyptus and sheep's hoofs around it. She said, "Half the Muslims in Sudan listen to music in private or in the secular clubs, the Nubian Muslims even sing and dance to Allah, so it makes no sense they would care about Harith's music. More than half our countrymen drink Aragi and Merissa (alcoholic beverages). Your Pappuh is doing something else to anger them. I see he writes letters that they don't like and he's talking too much...in public."

"It's about the trees!" I said and looked to Mommysweet for agreement.

Mahdi Pappuh had written papers complaining about the forestland up in the Sahel region and how the Nimeiri government was allowing the denigration of vast timber so that the wood could be turned to charcoal, which was our country's primary source of cooking and heating fuel. But then a pall came over Auntie's face and she looked up at Mommysweet and she said, "Jiddi--Harith is putting poison in his body."

Mommysweet didn't look surprised or alarmed. Her eyes told Ramah that she already knew and then they didn't speak about it, but unfortunately, I had heard that Mahdi Pappuh was putting "poison" inside his body and I became very worried. I cried and told them that I worried he might die and Ramah assured me that he would not die. She made up some story about it being "medicine to heal heartbreak." But it was in the course of that week that I began to notice a cryptic panic in Mommysweet. I felt that the devil was about to show up barefoot, with all ten dicks exposed, any day.

It was the first time that Mommysweet ever kept me out of school for an entire week. Auntie Ramah came over every day with her children (Ian and Liv) and we would all have picnics or wash clothes or sit by the river and tell stories. I could tell that Mommysweet was worried terribly about Pappuh, on the edge of her seat every second, but she knitted, cooked, sewed and kept her wits for me.

My faqih (teacher) eventually showed up to enquire about me, but Mommysweet did what she always did--stared blankly at the person, saying nothing as the person talked and talked, and then rather suddenly, in the middle of their sentence--she just walked off without even motioning goodbye. This was <u>always</u> embarrassing for me, because I was usually the one left to apologize and soothe the other party, especially at the Souq. I started saying what Pappuh told me to say: "My father forbids my mother to speak in public." This wasn't the least bit true, but Pappuh felt it better to just blame Mommysweet's notorious rudeness on him.

One night during that week, however, Mommysweet did speak. She came and woke me from my sleep, saying softly: "*Daughter...you must come and help mother to pray*." And I cried all the way outside--because my mother had actually spoken to me! I remember feeling so overwhelmed and honored, so incredibly shocked and exhilarated. I just couldn't wait for her to say something else, but of course, I knew by that age that it would be another year or so before she spoke again. Thus my tears were not only for having heard her beautiful, loving voice--but also for the agony of being made to long for it again. I thought it was very cruel.

Once outside the house, a tranquil Nile River night was upon us and Mommysweet took my hand firmly. I realized that we were going someplace, and this is what sobered me from my tears, because it was very unusual for women to travel at night, and without a man--unheard of. I also looked up and saw that Mommysweet was *topless*! Her little black breasts bare and pointy. My mouth hung open in a panicky fear, because although I had seen the southern and Nubian women of our country singing in the river and forests with their titties out, it wasn't something that Muslim wives did and certainly not northern women of Omdurman. We were neither southerners nor Nuba people, so I was terrified to see my mother topless outdoors, but Mommysweet pulled me along, my tiny feet padding just a little behind her as she floated serenely down the banks of the Nile river, an ivory headdress flowing down the satiny naked charcoal of her bare back.

Her sugary lyric replayed in my mind as much as I could play it and for as long as I could hold onto it: "*Daughter...you must come and help mother to pray.*"

Up ahead in the dark, we suddenly saw a crescent flock of candlelight.

As we got closer, I was stunned, because here were all the women of our Zarpunni (women's neighborhood), gathered together at the riverside...each of them *barechested* (!), their black shoulders high and proud. I tremble now remembering the sight of it--black women gathered in a secret otherness from Arab women and applying spiritual fellowship in a way that was naturally soulful and uniquely African as opposed to the confines and spiritual limitations of a Muslim or Christian prayer meeting. I must name the faces so that it is written: Auntie Ramah, Alek, Amina, Mariama, Naima (the dark wife of Said), Naima (the lightskinned one with honey-colored eyes, Waleed's wife), Auntie Eyoun, Auntie Assis, Naima (Fahid's wife), Rahel Om, Ingrid (who looked Palestinian but whose mother was a pure charcoal Nubian), Auntie Arek, Agom, Ponis, Karel, Ursula (from Ghana), Ajok, Opal, and my mother Jiddi.

Many children were there as well, all of us patiently still, respectfully quiet and in awe of the black river fire goddess our mothers had summoned simply by baring breasts and congregating in sickle fire and song.

"*Daughters will carry the heads of their mothers,*" sang Auntie Eyoun, the eldest Zarpunni, her muddy voice hurtling over the Nile River in broken, aching soul-bites. To which the other women replied in song, "*...mothers will color the eyes of the daughters.*"

I remember being astonished by the movement of Auntie Eyoun's buttocks. Truly, there is nothing in nature more connected, simultaneously, to the spirit world and to the sensual world...than the *Ass* on a black woman. That's just the truth. Everything about it--the shape, rhythm, the cushy-jello gravity of it guarantees that there will always be an us. And when I, as a six year old, saw those black women hike up their long skirts so as to walk into the Nile, and when I saw the seats of those skirts wrap around their buttocks lifting them high and tight--and when wet moonlight anointed their bare breasts and their womanly congregation of booty power shook the earth harder than cannons could--it was as if I were witnessing the actual birth of God and Man; of all humanity. I could not contain my joy at feeling...*free*! And I dashed into the river right behind Mommysweet and Auntie Ramah. I began dancing and singing and imitating the motherseeds, and although I had been told about the ancient Cushite women who bled their monthlies in the Nile for a thousand years, this had been the first time in my life that I could actually feel that the blood running in my veins was also the living dead (my ancestors) that run ever still in what Nilotic people call "*the river of blood.*"

Auntie Ramah led the Arab-Muslim prayer for my Madhi Pappuh to be returned safely to us. She threw rice as an offering. My Mommysweet led the prayer in ancient Nilotic Hebrew (the Cushitic language of the Nile river's original Black

Jews)...and Auntie Eyoun led the prayer in the language of the Nubians--Nobbin.

Opal banged the tambourine against her wrist and ululated to the moon as Auntie Ramah prayed God speed: "*...dearest one, creator of time* (dearest one; creator of time)...your sweet daughter, Jiddi, O Allah, who has been a good servant and a good wife, she is worried about the evil angels aligned against her husband. O Allah (o allah) --bring him home. Let him set foot on peaceful ground; let the quiet moon and tranquil river entrance his mind the way home...(The women*: say it/say it*)...and let him be as a King at his noble table, sweet Jiddi at his feet, until a ripe good age—Inshallah."

In the creed of the ancient Nubians, Auntie Eyoun said, "So let it be written...so let it be done." And in the song of the Nilotic Hebrews, Mommysweet sang, "Khu Sahu Sekem...buim mezuzah-shema."

I know that this night that I speak of is a big part of my becoming who I am today. It was the first time ever that I felt a strong sense of myself as being whole...*in the world (*but powerfully so*)*...a part of something more tangible and deeply rooted than merely my family or the community. In Africa, it's really true that the people aren't always able to notice themselves by skin color, because it seems that almost everyone, everywhere you go for your entire life--is black--Black is normal/everyone is black--*so you don't realize you're black* (being submerged in an all-black world is the equivalent of living in a race-less society). But on that night, I actually felt what being black *IS*, what being *African* is--and once I experienced the power of knowing the makings of me...moving in me...I felt indestructible...and could never be ambiguous again.

I remember taking Mommysweet's free hand and whispering to the moon, "Please bring my Pappuh home, Allah. I promise to be good forever."

~~

A week later, when Pappuh came home--he was mad at the government and high on drugs, but as always, he treated Mommysweet and I like dolls. He grabbed us, kissed us and twirled Mommysweet around in a soft dance. She cried. He unloaded a carload of fantastic gifts, and in fact, for Mommysweet--he brought an automobile! (Mommysweet would never learn to drive it and truly believed, according to Auntie Ramah, that automobiles, airplanes, radios, televisions, alarm clocks--even the Cobra/arh Theatre just blocks from our house--were possessed by demons). But just the same, Pappuh insisted that Mommysweet must learn how to drive in case something happened to him.

"Pappuh, where were you!?"

"In jail, Naima. This whole country is a joke, and yet they don't want anyone laughing out loud. I don't know why Africans don't rise up against the Arabs!" Of course, he himself was an Arab.

Anyway, he was home safely, and as African women, we began to spoil the King. Auntie Ramah cooked a Khosaf (raisins, figs and bananas in thick syrup with cream on top) and made a batch of Pappuh's favorite sweet--coconut cookies. His favorite meal, however, was baby lion's meat, pepper-brined and cooked over coals and served with a stack of Kisra dripping in honey and a stew we call Miris (sheep's fat, onions and dried okra). Unfortunately, it was tradition in our house that only Pappuh could prepare the lion's meat that we ate only on special occasions, maybe two or three times a year, so while Pappuh made the lion, Mommysweet and I made his next favorite dish--Sudanese Spicy Cherry Soup (an African gumbo). I write about it here, because of all the dishes we ever made for Pappuh, this was the one that would make cooking a permanent and extremely important part of Kola Boof's adult life. For it was Pappuh's praise and genuine regaining of strength after eating this particular meal that inspired me to always cook and to love doing it.

First Mommysweet made the base, which was water, sheep hoofs, garlic, onion, Khubz crumbs (a rich Arabian bread) and milk. Then she added Aseeda porridge and sugar. After that all blended, she put in crab legs, chicken, sheep's fat, a cup of Hilumur, potatoes, peanut butter sauce and a big bowl of ripe cherries with the pits still inside. On top of that came the spicy part--"*bom*"--red hot scorpion peppers from the Kababish tribe in Kordofan. Once that was cooking, she slit open an egg plant and seasoned it and baked it. She then had me serve Pappuh the Spicy Cherry Soup poured over the baked eggplant with thick wedges of Hopu (cornbread) and watermelon pickled in shata (hot sauce). He nearly died praising us! He talked about that meal for two weeks, it was so good!

As was our way, we prayed five times a day to the east--and above our house and the river--the sky was clear and white as the baby blue skies in Mommysweet's shoe box full of diamond chunks.

We were blessed.

~~

About a month later, I went to Mahdi Pappuh and asked, "Pappuh, can you please order Mommysweet to talk to me? She never talks."

"Oh, Naima. I cannot make your mother do anything. This is her house. Isn't it bad enough that I purchased her like a slave and took her away from her people, without her having any say in the matter? Isn't it bad enough that I forced her to learn Arabic and become a Muslim wife?"

"Then why did you do bad stuff to her, Pappuh?"

"I needed the right mud for planting sons. Your mother is a Waaq Oromo, the ancient tribe from Punt (Somalia) who gave birth to the Nilotics, the Nubians and the original Egyptians. Jiddi is the perfect woman, but she took revenge on me, you see. She killed all six of my sons but allowed you to live. If I am good to her, though, I have faith...she will let one boy slip through. I just know it."

"I feel so sad...that she won't talk to me. She and Auntie Ramah go for long walks and they talk in their language, but they won't teach me. They say that I will have a better life as an Arab Muslim. But I want to speak to Mommysweet."

~~

{*NOTE: Editors complained that a 6 year old would not speak as well as I write that I did in this autobiography. I submit that they're wrong and that I did speak, at five and six, just as articulately as I'm describing in this book.]

~~

"Come, Naima. You will go away again with Pappuh. We will have excavations in Napata and Meroe next month. My comrades in Islam will not know. We shall bring Aunt Kem (his helper from the Dinka tribe) and pretend that Aunt Kem is my maid and that you are her granddaughter. Of course, you'll have to take off from school, but what does a female need with education anyway? Is that good?"

"Yes, Pappuh!" I was ecstatic!

But who would have known that Mommysweet would have such a fit? Or as we say in America: She just went straight...*the fuck off.*

Pappuh begged: "Jiddi, it's only for three months!"

First, she removed her top so that her breasts were bare. Then her silence erupted into action.

She busted all the windows in the livingroom, flipped over the dining room table, smashed the ebrig into the wall and turned over the hutch! She kicked the back door out. She took a mallet and bashed dents into the car that Pappuh had purchased for her, which had sat next to the house collecting dust. She busted out the windows and threw rocks at the sun and the river.

She screamed high pitched "sounds," but no words. Sort of like those dog notes that American singer Mariah Carey used to make at the end of her songs, or like Minnie Riperton--that's what Mommysweet screamed out, only higher. You truly had to cover your ears, because I think that only dolphins can tolerate it.

I am certain that Pappuh would have given in and let Mommysweet have her way, but unfortunately, she did the thing that Nile river black women are known for--she bit him. In fact, she bit him so hard in the left shoulder and neck that he had to be hospitalized for two days. It was the first time I had ever seen a grown man cry. So for that viciousness, he insisted on taking me away to show Mommysweet who was boss.

I remember that Auntie Ramah came over after Pappuh drove off for the hospital, and I had been sitting on the porch crying while Mommysweet was gone topless, running down our river front screaming at the sun and cursing the river. Ramah slapped her across the face and hollered, "*Jiddi*!"

Later, when Mommysweet was tucked in bed and given tea with sleeping roots in it, Auntie Ramah came to me and explained why my mother didn't want me to go. She said, "Your father's on drugs, Naima. He's also in trouble with the government and with Islamic gangs in the North. He's complaining about the Arab financing of a gang war between the Baggara people and the southerners (Dinka,Nuer,Shilluck). Your mother fears that he will get you caught up in this trouble. As well as that--your father is a man and he's Arab. Your mother is a black woman, so she is *deeply* distrustful of Arab men, Naima. She believes that they have sex with their own daughters and sometimes kill them to keep it a secret."

Of course, Mahdi Pappuh would never do something like that and most of the Arab Muslim men that I grew up around were very loving, wonderful fathers to their children, but still, there were a lot of Arab Muslims who carried out honor killings against their own daughters. There were homes in which fathers and sons routinely had sexual intercourse with daughters and then stoned them afterwards. There were numerous incidents in which Arab men would take the little homeless Dinka, Nuer and Shilluk boys who begged in the streets for pennies and would sodomize those six and seven year olds as a kind of "sport" much like frequenting prostitutes. You have to understand that in our culture, the "*virginity*" of females (for the wedding night) is the highest protected and honored thing that there is--so sodomy of both wives and of children was a rampant occurrence as the lack of respect for women and lack of women's rights mixed with male supremacy and religious premium on the hymen--caused one of many "dirty little secrets" in our world. To Mommysweet (who hated Arab Muslim people, I was starting to realize), it just seemed like these incidents were more representative of Arab Muslim Sudanese culture than they actually were.

"Your mother loves your father," Auntie Ramah told me, "But she doesn't know him, Naima. She doesn't talk, because she lives in terrible fear of the Muslims and their ability to hear through walls. She believes Islam is evil, because the women are considered unclean and covered up as though they have a plague...which in our Oromo culture...is an abomination against God." The Oromo believed in *Gadaa*--the body of the woman and the circle of woman's self-determination and the woman's right to equal rule within the village of men. This, after all, was the reason why our ancient Oromo mothers had given up their own villages and agreed to live in the men's villages with men they were the *Gadaa-Kwilxxu* (womanists).

"But the Muslims," Auntie Ramah told me, "do not respect free women. We are separated into a Zarpunni (woman's place, women's neighborhood) that is ruled and dictated to by the men of the mosque. More than a thousand years, niece, Arab people have enslaved, raped and mutilated African women. They loathe blacks and have treated our children as the lower bowels of rats. The Arab, the Jew, the Caucasoid, the Spaniards and Latins, the people of India, the Foon (Asians)--they are *all* the bastard children of African slave women. This is why every race hates the African--it's because they come from us and cannot *get away.* They remain suspended in permanent niggerstock, but they want you to believe that we pure black ones are the niggers and not them. All of them are dirty piss-blooded trash; eternally lost. Pollution--the Caucasoids, the Arabs, the Jews, the Foon, the Indians, the Spaniards and Latins--all of them are nothing less than world pollution. *God...is a black man.* Do you understand me?" It was scary the way she whispered in hushed tones when she said "God is a black man"--but I nodded that I did understand, and then my auntie said, "God is a black man. You, Naima--are an African. Your mother's blood was pure enough to dominate the Arab blood. *tatu*, little one. Jiddi made you out of clay and baptized you in the Nile. You must not misunderstand your mother's rage. She is a Queen, Naima—a queen alone in a foreign land that is against her."

Auntie Ramah told me of "Caabudwaaq"--the great holy religious city of her and Mommysweet's race--the Oromo--the descendents of the Crow, the keepers of the coffee.

Then Auntie Ramah took me out to the river and we faced the setting sun as she carefully bared her breasts. I marveled noticing that her dusky pumpkin flesh was nearly identical to the dark orange of the fading sun. And then we prayed as ancient Africans would do...to the sun. "Our mother, the goddess Sudan," she taught me. "Our mother, the goddess

Sudan--for she *IS* the Sun. O kiss of God's wife, the lioness. Blacker than all black put together; Mah-mah."

~~

On the still-dark morning that Madhi Pappuh, Aunt Kem (the Dinka woman) and I set out for what would be his final archeological expedition, and the beginning, too, of our family's slow dissolve into the belly of evil angels, I fell asleep on the back seat of the jeep.

Mommysweet came to me in a dream--only it wasn't a dream. What I saw were more like memories of moments that had actually occured in our lives. Like the time Mommysweet had stood in the doorway of our home--too beautiful for words in a flowing curve-hugging cream lace goddessa gown, a single strand of bone white pearls clutching her pencil neck and her wild nappy hair loose. It seemed in the dream that I could actually taste the raspberry honey that she wore instead of lipstick on her lips (and most Africans don't need lipstick, they are born with separately colored or matted lips). I could smell the fragrance of her shoulders, Jovan Musk Oil, I believe from America. And on her cheekbones were painted intricate henna designs, a white tapestry against charcoal that highlighted the almond curve of her perilous eyes and covered her forehead like a veil. I could see her smiling at me again, just as she had on that day in real life. I could hear the song that was playing inside our house (and although I sung the words as a child, I had no idea what they meant). It was Nina Simone singing:

"*I put a spell on you! 'Cause you mines...a doop-doop dee*!"

Images carried me sleeping as the raspberry honey on Mommysweet's lips became a sweet juice in Pappuh's mouth and I could see his juicy dark heart beating like a glowing bunch of red tomatoes beneath shallow waters. Then I saw Mommysweet planted in the center of our livingroom floor, sobbing horribly--and this was another actual event from our real lives that I was re-dreaming.

She had spilled her box of diamonds all around her and sat looking inside them as though glimpsing some nostalgic photographs or Polaroids, but they were just uncut blue stones. Jagged, chunky, sliverous...iceburg white and sparkling clear. There was nothing inside them. I had been almost five and remember Mahdi Pappuh trying to get her to use speech to explain why she was so upset, but she wouldn't talk and kept crying, uncontrollably, so Mahdi Pappuh held her and rocked her and caressed the roughness of her hair for hours and hours until she finally fell asleep in the cave of his chest. She would be seemingly insane and pathetic--and then totally normal again the following morning.

In the dream, I next saw a beautiful boy behind the bushes. He was calling me.

His face was that "*Biblical Days Black*" color and his beckoning arm looked too skinny and too familiar. Of course, I went into the bushes with him--and there I saw Mommysweet in her flowing white goddessa gown, her face smeared by crying as she stood at the edge of the river just outside our house. There were these boys with her, each one reed thin and tall with a large oval head and satiny pretty charcoal skin. They waded into the Nile, their cold eyes dead as fish eyes—six beautiful boys.

~~

I jumped out of my sleep! Panting awake so as Pappuh looked down with concern. He said, "Just in time. We're almost at Atmu's house."

I had not been able to stare down the sorrow that tormented Mommysweet in my dream. I had not been able to bear it when she walked into the river behind them, her feet losing track of sanity and her beautiful raven's face submerged beneath the water's surface, her lungs lonesome with the dead echo of the boys.

Arriving in Khartoum, we dropped in to visit a good friend of my father's, a Turkish-Nubian archeologist named Atmu Bahri. I always knew him as Uncle Atmu and was well aware, even at that young age, that Uncle Atmu and my father had reached an agreement that I was to grow up and become the wife of Atmu's then newly born son, Micah. In fact, many times when we visited with Uncle Atmu, his pale white Arab wife would sadly and grudgingly hand baby Micah to my father, and then Mahdi Pappuh would hand the baby to me, admonishing, "Be careful now...hold his head just right...this is to be your future husband after all."

Nothing disgusted Atmu's wife more, but because the mother has no say, there was nothing she could do about her son being married to a black Arab girl with nappy hair.

Anyway, I'll never forget that morning when we arrived at Uncle Atmu's house, because the whole block had been descended upon by an army of shiny black crows (I kid you not)—dark as velvet and braver than the sun. Beautiful velvety black birds everywhere!

"*What the hell*!" Pappuh had cursed in wonder.

But I knew by the dream that it was Mommysweet.

For there is no way to escape an African mother's love, and those who are African or truly Black reading this book--*KNOW* what I'm talking about. This is why I kissed baby Micah extra gently on his soft beige forehead that day and did not resist when his tiny infant's hand wrapped around my fingers and gripped on to them for dear life. I had felt so loved, so cherished and adored when I saw the prestigious blackness of the crows Mommysweet sent to greet me. Holding the precious baby, I wanted to be a mother, too.

It was 1978.

The defining year of our lives.

That year...when the skies of Sudan were never bluer.

The beginning of knowing for me.

The beginning of that bittersweet march to my parent's bloody end.

I remember being a pretty little black girl, holding my arranged future husband, baby Micah, in my stick-bony arms and asking him in Arabic, "*...my baby hungry*?"

NIGHT OF THE LIVING DEAD

Our babies shall starve to bones--too weak to cry.
Our men will be lost inside the endless echo
of the wilderness they seek.
Our breasts will shrivel into drought--abandoned
and scorned.
And the whole world will not just witness it, but abide it:
we--"the night"
the living dead
for whom all Gods visit as a grave
because without our own God, no prayer
had a right
had a right

(Comb YOU Nappy Head...the crown...the PROOF
cada-doot, Egypt/cada-doot Nubian
Comb you Nappy Head/come back to life)

tima usrah means “through fire comes the family.” The “tima” represents the African race...it means, literally--”the result of great fire.” The “usrah” is the bloodberry of the ancestors; the wombs of the mothers; the crowns of the scalps—

the unification of the Nilotic flesh in all its black perfection. We call our hair--the one true hair--the *proof.* It is the nappy, wooly royal crown of our fathers and mothers—the unique mark that separates the African from all who came about to destroy him. This is the crown that validates him...and yet...my father did not have that crown, but still felt very strongly that he was a black man and wanted to rescue...the black people of Sudan.

It is very hard to explain to an American--exactly what and who is black in an Arab ruled African country like Sudan. We do have a very, very large number of ruling White Arab Muslims in Sudan, despite what you see on television or hear reported--they live in Khartoum, Omdurman, the North of the country, and they are the ruling elite, and during news coverage of the war and the genocide in Darfur, the Sudanese government did an excellent job of keeping our nation's White Arabs out of public view...but just as well...there are hundreds of thousands of black people in Sudan, who look as deep dark brown as Kola Boof or who look as brownskinned and ethnic as Black Americans, and most of them would slap your face and declare war against your house if you called them "*black.*" They consider themselves to be Arabs. Their dream is to transcend their African origins and someday become fully recognized as upstanding, fully golden-skinned (gold skin is white in Africa) Arab Muslims. Most of these are mixed-race Nubians of the northern Sudan who have suffered so much racism and religious persecution over hundreds of years of British Colonialism, followed by Arab Minority rule (which included massive rapes and racial profiling-type lynching) that they (the Nubians) have bought into the Arabism that teaches that Africans are inferior savages left over from prehistoric times.

I remember as a small child being taught this in school. Being told that black people are inferior to Whites (Arabs being classified as white in Sudan, not Caucasoids). We were taught that the whitest Arab was the highest and most beloved "son" in the eyes of Allah...and that the darkest, most charcoal colored "son" was the last remnant of Asli-Nalla's evil impurity as a woman (she, charcoal black Asli-Nalla, being the Cushitic-Ethiopian mother of the entire human race). Nubian men, the Arab Muslims taught us, could be tolerated if they submitted to Islam and married lighter women (which are nearly impossible to come by in Sudan) to produce less African babies, "lighter babies"...but the Dinka men, Nuer and Shilluks and other extremely charcoal colored men were seen mostly as hopeless (and yes, for Nubians who are reading this book--I do realize that the Nubians are also charcoal black in color, but there's only 100,000 Nubians left, and therefore, since they live in closer proximity to the Arabs, they were seen as easier to breed lighter, as they've been doing it for much longer than the South). The Dinka, Nuer, Shilluk, Azande and other Southern tribes were hated and considered "human stains" against the northern Muslim people's longstanding goal of transforming Sudan into an Arab country as lightskinned as Egypt; one that their Arab neighbors could look at with pride and reverence. Of course, it didn't help matters that the Nubians, Nuers and Shilluk were also predominately Naturalists or were Christian (from British Colonialism) and refused to submit to Islam or to Arabism. They insisted on clinging to their African heritage and worshipping their own God and their own trinity--God's goodness (the cattle) God's House (the Sun and the River are "churches" to Africans) and God's Wife, the Lioness (woman's bare breast and menstrual cycle), and because the ancient blue black Cushitic people's and Nubians were once Nilotic *Hebrews* who had believed in the sanctity of the women's menstrual cycle and women being topless (totally at odds with the Koran)--the Arab Muslims (who started out as invaders, not indigenous people) despised the true Africans even more.

From day one, the children of Sudan are conditioned from birth to abide by the differentials of hair texture, gradations of skin color, shape of lips and foreheads and tonality of the way one speaks Arabic. Only *good women* can produce *good people*, so that on the television and magazine covers of Sudan, a country where the overwhelming majority of people are ebony black to charcoal, there were never any black African women allowed on t.v. or in magazines--unless they were as old as elephants, big as a rhino and played, ever briefly, the maid, or were cast as bit-part prostitutes. Only the White Arab woman of the north or a Palestinian woman or Middle Eastern women were *good women* and only from them could goodness come:

night of the living dead

--coming dead from dark wombs

~~

It was during our visit with Uncle Atmu in Khartoum that I saw slaves for the first time in my life. Little charcoal Dinka children tied to the back doors of Arab Muslim houses just the way Americans keep pet dogs. In fact, this was why Mahdi Pappuh had stopped in. He wanted to see with his own eyes if it were true.

~~

And it was true--even as early as 1978.

A man named Abu Fayid Ali, an official of Sadiq al Mahdi's "Umma Pary" kept three Dinka child slaves. I was with Pappuh Mahdi when he and Uncle Atmu and about twelve of their other "human rights" colleagues (all Arab Muslim men), went to the man's house to confront him about it and got cursed and called *abeed-shafa* (basically nigger lovers) before the city police officials arrived to threaten Mahdi Pappuh and the group with arrest if they didn't leave this good, clean upper class Arab neighborhood in peace. We saw the slaves though--two boys, around ten or eleven and blacker than crude oil (the Dinka being the blackest people on earth, as well as some of the most beautiful), were chained on either side of the back door of Abu Fayid Ali's house and a little girl of about six (who looked to be their sister) stood inside the house, staring at us through the windows as though her greatest prayer was that either death would take her or that we would. Her tightly closed mouth spoke of unspeakable horrors, and yet the sky above us that morning was the most brilliant robin's egg blue that nature could produce.

"I pay my taxes, I go to mosque," cried Abu Fayid to his neighbors, as though he were being unfairly picked on. He was draped in something like a toga and his bone-faced Arab wife stood behind him screaming expletives from beneath her burkah. Her own caramel creamy children watched from a balcony at the top of the house--they didn't look to be skeletal or malnourished as the black Dinka children did.

The police said, "No one's breaking any law here. The man has servants." In Sudan--the law is religious, it's by Shariah, but very often--Islamic Scholars are not involved and the stupidest men rule via their personal prejudices and ignorance. There is no separation between church and state.

But anyway, this confrontation was particularly painful for Mahdi Pappuh, because he and Uncle Atmu had grown up with Abu Fayid Ali and once counted him as a close personal friend. I remember as we drove away from the house, Pappuh kept complaining to the other Arab Muslim men with us, "How can this be our same brother? How could he be doing something like this?"

I asked Pappuh, "Where are the parents of the Dinka children?"

"Probably at the bottom of a ditch," he said off the top of his head.

"No," said Kabir, one of the men in the back of the van. He told us, indignantly, "Only the father was killed. The mother was sold to a doctor in Egypt. They've had to cut out her tongue and chop off one of her feet to keep her from running away."

"This is a lie!" Pappuh cried out, furiously. "This is all a lie! I just do not believe it!" I stared at my father, noticing him so intensely that I thought I could hear the blood traveling in his head.

Uncle Atmu, who was driving, snorted and said something, which altogether was to the effect of: "Believe it my brother. I have not been lying to you all this time. Garang is not lying, either, with the stories he tells. There is a movement under foot. The government is paying people to get a war started. Didn't you read about the government complaining in the newspaper the other day about all the refugees pouring into Sudan from Kenya? Too many blacks, Harith. Gangs on horseback are being sent south to agitate the Dinkas and in Darfur, the same thing. When they come back, they bring the wives and children. They sell them to politicians and businessmen right here in Khartoum. A lot of Palestinians buy slaves, it's so cheap to purchase one. Saudi Arabians, Jordanians, Syrians, Iraqis, Iranians, Libyans, Yemenese--you'll find Sudanese women and children with their tongues cut out working in homes all over the Arab world."

"Is this what we've come to?"

"*Come to*!" shouted Uncle Atmu. "Islamic gangs have been murdering southerners every since the British left the Arabs and the Egyptians in control of this country. Look at the 1955 massacre in Torit. Look at the hundreds of Blacks who were decapitated by Arab gangs in Juba in 1965. Look at Wau in 1965...Arab Muslims poured gasoline over the heads of pregnant black women and set them on fire."

~~

Later that night, as Uncle Atmu's wife and Aunt Kem (the Dinka maid who traveled with us) served up dinner, there was a sudden sound from outside. Rocks pelting the house? Everyone was alarmed and everyone scrambled. I jumped up from the table and ran to protect my future husband--baby

Micah. Gently, as I heard a rock crash through one of the livingroom windows, I raised baby Micah out of his crib and held him close to my tiny body, my smallish hands tucking the blanket over his head and my reed thin voice humming a lullaby. Arab teens outside were shouting epithets and daring Pappuh or Uncle Atmu (the Arab Muslim "*nigger lovers*") to come outside.

Uncle Atmu's wife, being a mixed race Arabian looking Sudanese woman married to a white Turk (Atma was whiter than my father), did not appreciate her marriage welfare or baby Micah being threatened all for the sake of some worthless black *abeed* stock (her own black blood was something she conveniently never spoke of). She hissed like a snake, "See what you've done! All for your precious niggers!" And with that she rushed upstairs in a complete rage.

Only moments before, she and Aunt Kem--whose skin was pure charcoal--had been trading recipes and tending the place setting, and in that moment, I think it clicked in my mind what racism really is and how subtle and natural it can be inside a person. To look at Atmu's wife, one would perceive a slender, angelic-faced Muslim woman in a stunning Burkah, but in reality, she was the typical selfish, skin-bleaching racist mosque princess who wanted to be white.

Aunt Kem, of course, being such a proud Dinka woman of true class didn't pay the Arab wife any mind. She grabbed a sharp butcher knife from the kitchen and stood ready to fight with the men if it came to it. You can't imagine how black she was.

In my head as an adult, I see Aunt Kem retrieve that knife over and over again--the placid look of acceptance on her unbelievably black face. I always think of how delicate and pretty she was, and more than that, how she couldn't have cared less about being pretty.

Uncle Atmu turned the porch light on...and the Arab teenagers dropped their rocks and haul assed down the street hollering like a pack of hyenas.

To which Auntie Kem remarked, "Oh, good then, let's eat."

~~

We became nomads. Pappuh, Auntie Kem and I traveling from one archeological dig to the next.

As I was compiling my memories for this book and getting information from relatives who still live in Sudan and Egypt, my Uncle Kar (not his real name) asked me, "Don't you know how skinny your Pappuh had gotten the last months before the murder? Don't you remember how his face had shrunken and his hands turned skeletal? Don't you remember how the drugs made him foam about the mouth?

No, I don't. I suppose that being so young, I only saw him as what he presented to me--my hero and protector. My truth.

"Don't you remember how Harith couldn't stand injustice? He was ashamed to be around it. He hated being a white skin!'

Yes, I remember that; Pappuh cursing the government and most Arabs.

I remember Pappuh digging up fossils and pieces of pottery from the ruins in Napata (the ancient capital of Cush near the fourth cataract). Pappuh taking my hands and making me read the hieroglyphics at Nuri and El Kuru--and the way he yelled at me when he was digging at the ruins of the ancient Kingdom of Meroe. I had nearly peed on myself as he yelled, "There are more pyramids in Sudan than in Egypt, Naima! You must stop being a little girl and understand what I'm teaching you! Everything came from here--it came from the blacks! It came from your little black pussy!"

He was obsessed, angry and impatient with God.

It was during these few weeks that I really got to know who my father was. He was "*me*"...as I've become today (sans the drug use.)

~~

Uncle Kar: "*Let me tell you, Naima...it was when the British and the Egyptians succeeded in covering up the Nubian Valley that your father started losing it. They put a lake over the heart of Nubia and drowned a virtual universe of undiscovered archeological data, history and ancient artifacts...artifacts that your father saw as "the black roots" of Egyptian and Greek history. Harith fought an entire decade to stop the dam from being built! His whole life was one desperate attempt to save the black people of Sudan and to preserve their history--their greatness.*"

~~

In the 1960's, Mahdi Pappuh had campaigned mightily against the Sudanese government's creation of Lake Nasser/Lake Nuba--the largest man-made lake on planet earth. It conveniently covers the Nubian Valley on the Sudanese side and was responsible for the exodus of some 100,000 displaced Nubians who found their towns and villages submerged under water--all so the Arab Egyptians and the British could disconnect, as Pappuh claimed, the truth about the contributions of the Black Africans to the birth and glory of both Egypt and ancient Greece. Mahdi Pappuh believed that Nubia and Cush were the mothers of Egypt and Greece. It had been his life's dream to prove it.

Uncle Kar told me about verbal threats in the mid-sixties that had turned into actual beatings and death threats by the seventies: "*When they put in the lake*...your father attempted suicide. To him, it meant the end of authentic Nubian culture, and now that we're in the new century, Naima, I can tell you--he was right. The Nubian people have been dying off since the seventies. You can hardly find one who isn't breaking his neck to become an Arab Muslim by marrying out. The government still sterilizes some of their clanswomen."

"Still?"

Slavery, civil war, genocide. Mahdi Pappuh and other colleagues of his like Joseph Lagu, Lam Akol and Dr. John Garang (who was actually part of the Arab government when we knew him in 1978) saw it coming. Many of Pappuh's closest Arab Muslim friends (who have asked not to be named for good reason) say that my father predicted as early as the late sixties that the powerful Arab North would never accept total equality and brotherhood with the poverty stricken heavily Christian African South. He used to say, "The Muslims won't feel Muslim until they kill off the Christians. That's just the nature of all religions."

"But we're Muslims, Pappuh."

"Only because it's safer."

By the year 2002, the United States Secretary of State Colin Powell would call Sudan, "The single worst human rights nightmare on the planet."

~~

In retrospect, I truly believe that we northerners knew about what was in store for the southerners long before they did. This is the only way that I can explain the blank stare that I get from many Sudanese expatriots whenever I mention the fact that the slave raids and "false jailings" of certain liberal-minded Arab Muslims were already taking place when I was a little girl in Omdurman during the late seventies.

I tell them about being with my Pappuh Mahdi on his archeological tour in 1978 and witnessing the rounding up of the Nuer people by Arabs on horseback and they say--"no, that started around the mid-eighties." But they're wrong. The divergent Arab Muslim political parties who would do battle to become Sudan's present day terrorist regime were already enacting their campaigns of racial hate (we should say *colorist* hate since so many of the Arabs are black themselves) against the Black African southerners in 1978. Not only did I witness this rounding up, but I also overheard many Arab Muslim liberals come to Pappuh and complain about the similar incidents. Their Nubian maids and houseboys were suddenly being refused service at supermarkets or denied driving privileges for no legal reason or just plain beaten up in the streets by Arab soldiers.

Unrelated to race, but certainly a sign of the coming anarchy, was the day that Uncle Kar joined Pappuh on a dig near the fourth cataract. He and I decided to walk to the open market to get something for lunch...and on the way back, we came across one of the most horrid and unshakeable memories that I have in life--the sight of a group of Arab Muslim brothers (black ones) kicking and berating one of the men's wives for bearing only daughters and no sons. Uncle Kar being the man he is, he couldn't just pass and do nothing. He had me stay behind as he went over and argued with the men. He tried to talk to them about the will and word of Allah. He used stories of the Koran to plead for fair treatment of the woman (she looked mixed race and extremely light, my father's color)--but his plaintiff good works only brought out more evil in the men. They doused the wife and mother with gasoline and set her on fire!

Right in front of us, in broad daylight.

I cried for two days straight and Madhi Pappuh yelled at the police officials until he was blue in the face, asking them, "*What is Sudan coming to*?"--but nobody cared. She was just a woman, and worse than that--an Arab woman who had failed to give birth to sons, which in any Muslim society automatically makes a woman *nothing*.

Pappuh was next.

A few soldiers (police or whatever they were) showed up at our dig site one morning and kicked sand in Pappuh's face as he slept. They warned him that "*the evil eye*" was going to be turned on him. In our culture, the evil eye is a very serious thing. It means almost literally..."death is upon you."

Pappuh being an Egyptian should have taken it more seriously.

Several co-workers at the dig told Pappuh, "Move your family to Kenya. Go to Europe. Move to Ethiopia."

"I am a warrior like Mohammed," was Pappuh's reply. "Allah will protect me."

But Auntie Kem told him many times, "The only people who like you, Harith, are the goodhearted ones. Those are terrible odds."

~~

We went home and Uncle Kar returned to Egypt.

I imagined Mommysweet as a black crow presiding over the porch and couldn't wait to see her beautiful face again and to be wrapped up in her bosom of love. She was the best mother in the world and that's all I truly thought about as we drove the roads back to Omdurman.

Just like in Napata and Meroe and in the road where the gasoline-soaked woman burned to death...and on the city street where black children spent their childhoods as slaves tied to the back doors of rich men's houses--*the blue sky followed us.*

~~

I am an orphan--a lost girl. It was the blue sky that created me.

night of silence/Silent night...night of the living

Even on that night when my parents became a part of the next world and could no longer abide me. It was the insanity of the blue sky that kept me calm. I was calm because...I knew it would come back again...Sudan's blue sky (the insanity). Others who come from third world countries, like I do, will know exactly what I am talking about. And they will admit that there's no way...not to know.

~~

We went home and the soldiers were waiting for us.

Mommysweet, just as I imagined, was there presiding over the porch of our house. Her black velvety crow-like countenance rising up into the shape of a menacing hooded cobra; her mahogany eyes, braver than the sun, summoning us home.

Auntie Ramah was in jail--accused by some local Arab women of being a lesbian. One of them, Nasiiba, claimed that Auntie Ramah had put a spell on her that made her dream every night of she and Ramah cuddled and licking--"like snakes."

The authorities at the jail wanted to question...*me*.

I knew, from staring into Mommysweet's eyes, that they wanted to take me into a back room and terrify me into saying something horrible and untrue about my relationship with Mommysweet's dearest friend. And then they would have the blood of a child as an excuse to publicly stone my aunt in the streets.

Pappuh forbid it. He said, "You're not asking my daughter shit! She doesn't know anything about Ramah's grown woman's life. She's a little girl. And you get the hell away from my wife!"

I think we all knew that Auntie Ramah was a lesbian. Surely, we did. Even as young as I was, I knew without being told--her children knew it. It's just that we didn't have a particular word for it (as children), there was no reality or idiom for such a state of being--to Africans who were not Muslim or Christian, it was "natural flux"--a natural part of nature like catepillars turning to butterflies or crocodiles building nests, and hence, all around us, there were certain men and women that the old high priests of the rivers and swamps would have called "*Flower Children*"--people whose ancient root spirit was neither male nor female, but one half of each, so that they were special angels from the world of the Cushite Sky Gods. Or at least this was how Africa's non-conquered spiritual folks saw things (it's much like that in India, too, where they hold Eunuchs and hermaphrodites as "saints")--the fear and hatred of these gay people is not African in the least, but comes from outside invaders (the Europeans, the Arabs, the Christians and Muslims)--and this is really true, because the indigenous religions of Africa, the river and sun people, the ancient Nubians and Egyptians, they all saw it this way--*Some People are just gay.* I guess you call it "Pagan."

And I, Kola Boof, am not gay or bisexual, but I'm just telling you that before Islam and Christianity, Nilotic African people did not fear, hate or persecute homosexuals.

In my childhood, many times, if we should happen upon two women bathing in a loving way at the river or see boys playing the secret "size" game that boys play (boys will be boys), or if we happened upon the Muslim clerics and their well known penchant for sodomy--then we were to pretend that we had not seen what we had seen and erase it from our minds. And let me just say that if you think the Catholic Priests are something with regard to molestation and sodomy, then your minds would be blown by the rampant sexual acts among Muslim religious hierarchy in the name of "purity" and "chastity" over in Egypt-Sudan. Somehow...very unfortunately, these religions such as Christianity and Islam have made sex and sexuality into something dirty, something sinister and evil--and in turning sex into amputating God's genitals--they have created a world of perversity.

And in Sudan, if you told someone that you had seen a sexual act at the creek or in the forest or anywhere--they would only act as if you were stone and warn you about the public ostracism that accompanies people who hallucinate things. Black African river/sun people didn't want to discuss sex, and frankly found the subject boring--they had a "*been there, done that*" attitude and would look at you like: "don't you know human nature?" They also felt that sex was "personal" between two consenting adults and felt dirty just talking about someone else's sexual habits. The Arabs, Christians and Muslims, however, took a different view. They saw sex as evil, and furthermore, they saw homosexual sex as unnatural and sought to eradicate it from human nature.

My auntie Ramah, the person who raised me more than Mommysweet did, was a lesbian and a good mother. She was a loyal, committed friend to my parents (Pappuh adored her!), and she was a truthful, nurturing, healing influence on my childhood. Before her husband was killed she had been a caring, attentive wife (although even back then, Pappuh and Uncle Kar said she should never have been with a man--but women are forced to in our culture, you don't have a choice). Auntie Ramah was a wonderful cook, a talented seamstress. And now that her husband was gone, she and her accuser, Nasiiba, had become like two moons rotating around some intoxicating forbidden world.

"I won't have my daughter set foot in any man's jail!"

"We have orders to see the Mullah at once!"

Pappuh was livid. "Then you tell him to come to my home! But I will not have my child interrogated in some jail. And not out of my presence. You go back and tell your Mullah who I am...I'm an Arab man--an Egyptian! A Muslim father! I am *Harith Bin Farouk*! You make sure he knows who he's dealing with. Now get the fuck off my land and stay away from my wife!"

Within the hour, the tiny squat investigator from the jail was pulling up in front of our house. Name of Ali (I shall write this as best as I can remember it).

Pappuh jumped up from the kitchen table and literally flung himself outdoors.

Mommysweet, who was at the stove, looked at me with worry. I followed her as she hurried out to the porch.

"You're aware of the *murahaleen* are you?" the tiny fat man asked Madhi Pappuh threateningly. He had four soldiers with him.

We had heard of this swarm--*murahleen*--a title used by the Dinkas and other southern blacks to describe renegade Arab Muslim horsemen (usually far from our area)--killing parties who went to the homes of black southern religious and political leaders and put them out of the world.

"How do you know that I'm not one?" Pappuh shot back.

"Oh, you're not a real Muslim brother," said the investigator with disgust. "You're a traitor to Sudan, Harith. A traitor to Allah and an ape worshipper--just look at your wife."

Pappuh rushed at him--but the soldiers caught him in a net of arms and chests.

As they held Mahdi Pappuh and kept him from swinging a punch, the investigator said something to my father that people have said to me all my life--"You talk too much." He said to Pappuh, "You use the fact that you're an Arab Egyptian, a white man...a Muslim. You use all these cards to do your crooked bidding against jihad and the true brothers. But your days are short, Harith--the evil eye is upon you."

That was all...that needed to be said. The little man turned around and went back to his jeep. He was gone as quick as he had come.

If I had known back then what the full weight of those words were--I wouldn't have been able to keep food on my stomach. I would have worried about it every waking moment. But I did not, at that time, really understand the seriousness.

Or that my parents would be killed that very night.

We ate dinner (what it was, I don't remember).

I overheard Pappuh telling Mommysweet that we should pack up in the morning and "*take a vacation*" to Ethiopia or Kenya. He seemed to think that we had plenty of time. He kept talking about *in the morning*.

Mommysweet, as usual, said nothing. But she doted on me every ten minutes. I remember that she was so glad to have me home and that she looked so...pretty. Her slender wand of a hand would pass me sugar cubes or pat my shoulder or run over the jungle thickness of my bushy African hair. I was given actual chalk (like they use on blackboards) to draw things with, which back then, was my favorite thing in the world.

I think I drew animals all over the stones in the backyard.

And then...just as darkness fell...*Auntie Ramah showed up*!

I felt her coming before I saw her.

Her heavy feet were ambling up the river's edge, her mouth moaning just a little and her body badly bruised from where the jailors had beaten her. I jumped up, saw her coming, and then ran yelling for Mommysweet and Pappuh to come--Auntie was home! She had her children, Ian and Liv, with her. I just knew that Mommysweet would finally be moved to speak, say something to Auntie Ramah. That's really what my excitement was about.

It hurt me...to my heart...to see Auntie Ramah standing before us that night.

Her right eye blackened and swollen shut, her lip busted, her pretty orange skin covered in purple puffy blotches. She told us that she had been blamed by religious officials (both Muslim and Christian) for the birth of two sets of twins--both born on the same night and both born in Ramah's section of Omdurman (in our world, amongst many different ethnic groups, the birth of twins is seen as a curse or a warning from God that the community as a whole is not worthy of "grace"). Since Auntie Ramah was both a witch and a lesbian, many people thought that it must have been her who brought bad luck and caused two sets of twins to be born, but when the soldiers fetched the four newborns from the hospital and brought them to the jail and had Ramah hold each one--not one of them cried. So they released Auntie promptly and a different neighborhood witch was picked up.

"I just wanted you to know that I'm alright," she told us, as Ian and Liv held her hands tightly, their dark faces petrified with terror and their cheeks wet from crying. They had already lost their father, so the thought of losing Ramah was more than they could bear. They loved and needed their mama as tremendously as I did my parents. And I have come to know that this is the thing that really makes us children...needing and being protected by adults who love us is what makes us children, not youth. For without parents, there is no foundation, no etiquette. Humans can be grown at any age. People in Africa know this, because thousands of "children" wander autonomously throughout the poor countries (I'm not saying that this is right--I'm saying that it's true), learning survival techniques, having sex with adults and earning a living...as young as nine and ten, running households and protecting other children. So, truly, it was a blessing for Ian, Liv and me to even have parents who loved us, protected us and looked after our childhood innocence. We were given the opportunity to be *children*, which...I would like to stress to the western world...is a luxury and not a privilege.

Mahdi Pappuh and Mommysweet gave Auntie Ramah warm hugs.

"Goodnight," said Auntie Ramah.

But, to my disappointment, Mommysweet didn't speak a single word and Auntie and her children walked off into the night, the children literally holding their mother up.

~~

There are some people who, throughout my life, have been brave enough to ask me the one question that I always hate to be asked.

"*What was it like to hear the murder of your own parents--how did it feel*?"

Well.

It was so overwhelming and so traumatic...that I can only describe it as being like a kind of birth. The world was confronting me with the reality that I was powerless to save that which I loved above all else. The reality that love, even the purest love of a child, can be placed in a box and marked nothingness. *No power*. I felt the most...unbearable horror. I hated my heart for continuing to beat. I couldn't believe in anything. I call it the "living dead," because in that morning--it was like a birth. I went downstairs and walked into the backyard where the bodies lay, and heard the sound of their blood seeping into the soil as if that were where it had come from...there was nothing else left in life for me to be afraid of. The very worst that could happen had happened. Like you can feel when your feet are going numb--I felt myself becoming fearless. The fearless ballad I told you about. I literally thought I was going to fly away. And more than anything else, I wanted to go with them wherever they were, I wanted to die, too. In fact, for many, many years after that moment (until I'd had my children), I don't think I'd wanted anything else.

That's what fearlessness is--being *ready* to leave this life behind.

And that was how it felt.

~~

Mommysweet tucked me into bed. I couldn't make out her features in the dark, because her velvet face was so black beside the moonlight spilling through my window as she leaned in and kissed my cheek and forehead. She said nothing, of course, nothing at all. She was just glad to have me back with her...where I belonged.

Goodbye Africa

All night and into morning and up until noon I sat on the front porch of our house, not knowing what to do. Pappuh and Mommysweet's bodies lay in the backyard like crash dummies resting in blood that had long dried to black and now glued them to the ground.

~~

All through the night, I had stayed near them to feel their warmth, to listen to their blood as it gathered to touch beneath the earth, and most of all, to feel for them in the silence--*to listen for them.* But come morning, I could not bear the sight of them. I don't like daytime anymore. In daylight, they seemed like dead bodies, whereas during the night, they had been almost alive; their blood hot and fluid as thoughts. They looked in the moonlight to be asleep--in a sleep so deep that not even dreams could find them.

I was seven years old. I sat there crying...waiting for my parents to wake up.

I replayed the last lesson that Mahdi Pappuh had been teaching me over and over in my head--*that jihad would not stop until establishing* Khilifah (the worldwide domination of

Islamic rule) *and that the evil eye was trained on Dar al-Harib* (the place of war; the South)....and that the five nations of ancient Nubia had been Wawat and Iretjet at the 1st Cataract, and then Yam, Kush and Medijay at the 3rd-5th Cataracts.

My parents were dead.

I knew that I should run and get help, but I was afraid to leave the bodies. I feared that someone would steal them.

It wasn't until noon that someone finally came by the house. It was the little cinnamon brown Arab boy who sold us the grain that Mommysweet used for making bread. He himself was no more than ten or twelve.

He came up to me, I told him what happened, and then he dropped his sack of grain and ran off quick to get Auntie Ramah.

When Auntie Ramah came back with the boy, she was out running him. Her shrieks and screams pierced the day like bolts of lightning. She ran right up to the porch, scooped me up in her arms, and then kept right on going until we were out back where the bodies were. She cried, holding me close to her, her sight impaired by the one eye being swollen shut from the police. She cried and screamed and cursed the universe and shook her fist crying.

~~

The authorities were called. Then they got in touch with Uncle Kar in Cairo. He volunteered to drive down from Egypt and fetch me so that I could live with my father's mother--Grandmother Najet. Auntie Ramah and I both tried to persuade the authorities and my Uncle Kar that it would be better if I stayed with Ramah and was raised up with her children in Sudan, but Uncle Kar and some of my other uncles insisted that I should be raised in my father's religion (Auntie Ramah was not a Muslim, was a witch--and a lesbian, and everybody knew it) and that I should be brought to Egypt where my flesh and blood relatives could keep an eye on me. Grandmother Najet, who I really didn't know very well at all, had already made arrangements for the bodies to be wrapped and transported to the family mosque in Egypt. Uncle Atmu of Khartoum also had a say in my fate, suggesting strongly that I be raised Muslim in Egypt so that I would turn out a proper wife and mother for his son, my future husband, baby Micah.

It was too much, because Auntie Ramah was already like a second mother to me. She had been one of the women who helped deliver me from Mommysweet's womb. It was she who had often times oiled my scalp and braided my hair so that Mommysweet could catch up on laundry or prepare some complicated recipe. And I knew what Mommysweet would have wanted--she would have wanted Ramah to raise me, because she couldn't stand Grandmother Najet.

On the morning of the day that Uncle Kar was to pick me up from Auntie Ramah's house, I got up before dawn and snuck back home---(notice the word "*snuck,*" a word that I would soon learn from my Black American family). The windows and doors were boarded up by then, but I knew a secret way to enter the house from underneath Mommysweet's verandah (on the other side). I came up through the dining room and then rushed upstairs to the secret hiding place where Mommysweet kept her shoe boxes full of diamonds. When I opened the boxes, the diamonds looked big and glowing, sparkling like ice cubes, some of them big as my eye balls. Obviously, being a child, I had no idea of the humongous fortune in the boxes. To me, they represented Mommysweet's pain and her beauty (without charcoal, Pappuh had taught me, the earth can't produce diamonds). For within their prisms, Mommysweet had entrusted all her secrets and prayers. I emptied them into a grain sack and ran back to Auntie Ramah's house before anyone woke.

After breakfast, Auntie Ramah did my hair up in what Black Americans call "afro-puffs" with a part down the middle (having this negroid hairstyle instead of being covered in a burkah would obviously infuriate my Uncle Kar). She put a thin layer of Vaseline on my face and fingered some in my nostrils for protection against the desert ride and scooped out some vanilla Halva/Tahinia (Sudanese candy paste for kids) and spread it over thin slices of bread so that I would have a sweet snack on the long trip to Egypt.

Auntie Ramah did not want to see Uncle Kar. She had put my bags on the front and had told him that I would be sitting there waiting when he arrived. So it was when she set me on the front steps with a jug of tea juice that we finally said our goodbye.

I gave Auntie Ramah the sack of diamonds. I lied and said to her, "Mommysweet told me to give these to you."

Her eyes filled with tears as she said, "Jiddi's rocks? I just assumed the soldiers had looted them. But here they are...with you. Come, Naima, quickly...we must go back to your house and honor your mother properly."

We went back to the house and stood on the banks of the Nile. We kissed each other and every diamond before tossing it as far as we could into the river of blood.

We said (in Nilotic Hebrew) the words of Queen Nefertiti's favorite hymn: *Khu sahu sekhem...enam betonim...onu ta ba*

~~

My Auntie Ramah knelt down beside me. She took my chocolate hands into her orange-brown ones. She said these exact words, "No matter where you arrive in the world...you must never forget who you are. You were born in March, which is the only time that when the female crocodiles of the Nile build their nests. The day of Alu, Goddess of Trees--March 3rd, 1969. You are born under the crocodile and Goddess of Trees."

I didn't want to hear goodbye, but her stare commanded me as though I were expected to be fully grown for a moment.

She said, "You are Naima...the one who is victorious; the one who is praying. Now *Say it*."

"I am Naima...the one who is victorious. The one...who is praying."

Water stood in Auntie's brown eyes, but she wouldn't let it fall. She nearly barked at me.

"You are the *tima*...the African...the result of great fire. You come from a people...you come from a place...you come from a nation!"

I come from a people...I come from a place

I come from a nation!

"You are the Naima Sijira of Omdurman. Bint il Nil (daughter of the Nile)."

I am the Naima Sijira of Omdurman. Bint il Nil (daughter of the Nile).

When she stood up, her face full of rage and her bitter voice admonishing me, "Don't you ever forget what happened here!"...I suddenly saw her in the ancient image of the Nile's greatest queen...the one the southern blacks called Nuku, God's Wife of Amon...the black woman who ruled Egypt dressed as a man, built the world's greatest library and took only African men from her royal army to be lovers. Indeed, the one who is regarded by historians as the only brave and mighty warrior ever to rule Egypt as both Queen and Pharoah (sometimes wearing a beard)...Queen Hatshepsut.

I love you, Auntie Ramah.

Thank you for my courage; thank you for my "womanist" spirit.

I have remembered everything you told me.

~~

I was alone in the world now.

Each day of my life...became a new heartbreak.

At the funeral, for instance, I found out that I was not an only child--*I had two brothers*! And they were both older than me. Their mother was a striking ebony black Ethiopian woman named Amina Kentworth (Afwerki). She had enormous eyes and kept her head shaved completely bald to denote Nilotic femininity. I would find out as an adult, from Uncle Kar, that she had been Mahdi Pappuh's mistress since around 1965, but had only seen him twice a year. I thank God that Mommysweet never knew. At the funeral, my brothers glared at me with a chilling hate--they resented me, I think, because Pappuh was always in my life and never in theirs. They were handsome boys, too. Very tall, as I am, with deep dark chocolate skin and fine boned faces. They were about ten and eight. As I was introduced to them, I tried to kiss one but his mother damn near slapped me...forbidding my uncles to even divulge the names of the boys to me. She said that I was not to be in their lives, *ever*. And to this day, I am not (although we know each other).

I watched the Arab townspeople carry Pappuh and Mommysweet into their tomb, and was finally hit, in that moment, with the realization that they were not coming back. They really were dead.

I cried all the way back to Grandmother's house and I cried all night.

There was nothing anyone could do.

My parents were dead and I had gained and lost two brothers all in one day.

I began to suspect that God hated me.

~~

And then in a few weeks, I had proof that God hated me.

Grandmother Najet, being an Arab Egyptian woman who had spent decades carefully weaning the blood of darker races out of her family line (my late grandfather had been Turkish-

Syrian Egyptian), felt that my complexion was a serious threat to the image of the House of Kolbookeks. People could see that I was actually related to the family and not just a servant's child or a slave girl. I had Pappuh's face, only 20 times blacker, and they could tell by my Arabic and the proud bearing and my aristocratic gait that I was "black blood" in the house, and that, of course, could bring Grandmother's pedigree down a few notches--she wouldn't be able to turn her nose up at the Nubians and Black Egyptians she encountered in the community anymore.

So she decided that I should be...*let for adoption*.

Her own grandchild.

~~

This is the only thing in my life that I cannot write about in detail, because...it is the one thing that very nearly killed my spirit. There are no words to describe how it feels to have one's own family scorn one's skin color, facial features and hair. To reject and withhold love based on a human being's failure to be something other than "fashionably ideal." And, as I leave this moment in my life alone (because I don't have the courage to explore the pain of it--which has not eased over the years), I will say that there is great wisdom in the proverb--"*That which does not kill you...makes you stronger*."

I was nobody's child.

~~

A Caucasoid man (the first white skinned man I'd ever met) showed up to take me away--and I was petrified! I remember being...*so* terrified and frightened. I was clinging to my grandmother's leg, crying and screaming, begging the whole family not to let the scary white man take me away. I was just a kid and with my fertile imagination he seemed mysterious like a space alien or some kind of jinn who ate the children that nobody wanted.

As it would turn out, he was a wonderful man and would become like a father to me. But still, the trauma and shock of it was cruel beyond words and has never left me. I kicked, screamed and hollered...but the yellow ones still placed me in his arms and watched complacently as he carried me out of the Kolbookek house and placed me in his car and drove away--as though I were some stain that wouldn't come out of the carpet. And being black, I guess I was.

But the real violation...was that I was leaving Africa.

Boarding a great fire bird...*being taken. From my body.*

From

LONG TRAIN TO THE REDEEMING SIN

Boy Magic

a love story

It happened all the time. Nuntandi got it in her head that she could order her own fate and even went and borrowed shoes from the village schoolteacher (she didn't want to wear the ones her Aunt Sula offered, because Sula was dying from what rural African men call *'the women's disease'*)...with which to defiantly walk towards that fate. Off to the city, off to the white women's favor room in a building in that progressive East African city, Nuntandi sojourned, a full days' walk, until she ended up in front of a municipal judge...told him she'd been raped and by whom...and then found herself; like so few young women brave enough to make such an accusation publicly...arrested and imprisoned.

"I demand," threatened Nuntandi's white lady, Helen Gator, "that something be done about this matter. If not, I will go to the regional assembly myself. The human rights of this poor girl have been violated! She was raped by her employer."

A Nyoro woman named Ijobi translated the white lady's words into a language that Nuntandi could understand.

Nuntandi's last name revealed that her father's bloodline wasn't of the same tribe of most of the decent families in this country. Her father was a full-blooded Acholi--considered a lower class breed of Africans known for their notorious lying, stealing, laziness and general unworthiness as human beings. In fact, it was a disgrace that Nuntandi's mother had lowered her status by marrying something so niggardly as an Acholi.

Pungent heat and a few flies whirled beneath the whirling blades of the courtroom fan. The judge's face looked like a charcoal kite under a white wig of thundering cotton.

"We have to check you for diseases," the Judge informed Nuntandi on that first day. "Not only that, but your employer is a very respected and well-liked man from India. We must make sure that you have not slandered his good reputation. Lock her up."

"Don't worry," said the white woman as Ijobi translated. "I will do everything I can to prove your case!"

Nuntandi, barely seventeen, merely stared at the 'out of place woman' blankly. Her crisp African hair and young, parched flesh were drenched in sweat, but in her deep eyes...there was a filled-in kind of warming. So optimistic and secretly triumphant that it could only be called, when residing in the barefoot gaze of a teenaged girl--*boy magic* (first love).

Six Months Later:

Helen Gator arrived at the women's dungeon (situated under the much larger men's jail) just in time to hear the loud protesting of Nuntandi's cellmates. Quickly, the white woman hurried down the damp, poorly lit corridor of stone, mud and straw...her senses quite used to the stench of diarrhea by now, but her eyes never quite adjusting to the casual ricochet of resident rats or the sooty mud-clay faces of women and girls who had been jailed indefinitely for nothing more than stealing a slice of bread to feed their children or for prostituting their bodies to *earn* that slice of bread...or for revealing that someone had raped them. One woman was even in jail for having written a poem that had angered soldiers passing through her village.

"Filthy rotten Acholi girl!"

"Nuntandi?" called out Helen worriedly.

"She stinks!" spat a cellmate. "Under the skin she stinks!"

"Rotting inside," remarked another woman who sat on the cot staring at Nuntandi with bolted, mournful eyes. Being a mother who had lost her husband, four sons and two daughters, she could only shrink inward to her bones and mumble, "...it's the women's disease."

Nuntandi stood off to the side, her legs skinny and wobbly as knot-bones, her dark left arm showing a small trickle of flaking scabby-white sores, and her gums, whenever she spoke or smiled, white with a creeping paste. Helen realized that Nuntandi probably had AIDS, but the court had refused to pay for any tests, and not only that, they still hadn't began any proceedings whatsoever to have Ghandi Mephisto brought in on the charges of having raped his employee. Forget it.

At this point, Helen's only real goal was to get the girl released from jail and returned to her village. Certainly, the baby couldn't be born in jail, and until she accomplished her client's release, Helen Gator wouldn't be able to sleep at night. Helen took twenty cents out of her pocket and paid one of the cellmates to translate a conversation between Nuntandi and herself. She now faced the girl with that familiar caucasoid expression of deeply projected remorse and pity. "Nun-tawn-diii?"

"I want Kimba," Nuntandi told her from behind the bars. The girl's face, to Helen, seemed strangely bony-chic and *exhausted* by being--as if a vision cast in mud. It seemed, still, that the poor thing was in love. Absolutely fueled by it.

"You find Kimba," Nuntandi told Helen for the hundredth time, resting her fragile hands over the protruding lump that was her pregnant belly.

"I went to your village," Helen began in frustration, fighting back the tears, but Nuntandi did not let her finish. The girl insisted, "If I am alive...then somewhere you'll find him. Kimba Kamilhgo, my kabaka; Kimba who loves me."

Those tears escaped Helen's pale blue eyes causing Nuntandi to giggle. Astonished by the tears and amused, she told the 'out of place woman,' "Don't cry. You haven' t found him yet."

Then the woman on the cot, the older one who had lost her family to AIDS and whose hair was straightened and wild and whose face looked like a monkey's face with deep, dark ritual markings in it, looked up at the white lady and told her, "Go look in all the sinful, sordid places. The kind of places where your Jesus Christ would go. In the company of death, it would be far better that you bring the girl's boy magic...than to waste your out of place...space."

Death Comes to Children:

Nuntandi lay on the cot where the women tried to keep her bones and flesh from shaking. Her brow, as it sweat, they wiped it, and when she lost vision at times...they forgave that she was the daughter of an Acholi and held her crispy head of hair in their laps and sung her traditional songs that her mothers and grandmothers had known and sang. It was made all the easier for the women to comfort the young girl this way...because of the crazy smile that seemed as a ritual scar on the young girl's face. A foreign tongue.

"*What dialect is this?*"

"He came in the cassava season," Nuntandi whispered at times. Her sight failing and the light trapped inside her heart and lungs shining over bare, in-held reflections of the tall, very black and beautiful young man called Kimba. His African man's ivory smile and all the power of his collected family's eyes suddenly encapsulating Nuntandi all over again. She had felt so tiny that day...flashes of heat covering her flesh in deep wavy cowlicks every time he looked at her.

"*She's speaking in 'Makkutandi'...her mother's tongue.*"

"I worked in his uncle's garden," Nuntandi whispered to her cellmates in the hopeful darkness. "The garden of Ghandi Mephisto. And when he came to his uncle's altar after fighting the revolution--he found me in the sun. I was covered in sweat and had my basket over my head and neither my feet nor my breasts were covered as a Christian's. And he liked it, the way that I had shaved my head and marked Kabaka Sengendo (a river God) virgins around it in white dots. I got water from the pond for him. And he had an illness about his bones, but he was the most beautiful thing that I had ever been looked at by. He drank it. He drank it down as if no girl had ever gotten him water before. Said his mommysweet had named him Kimba."

Black able hands tucked the raggedy blankets around Nuntandi's trembling body and began praying for the unborn. A light humming of song. For the baby.

But the bars of the jail could not hold Nuntandi back. She was out and beyond the will of her fate. Dancing. Covered over from head to toe. Picked up and moved. And someone saying, "This baby could be Jesus Christ coming back!"

Walk In the Light:

"I wanted to be a dancer," mumbled Nuntandi as sleeping sickness burst center-link in her giggling.

In her village, she had already been not only a dancing queen, but one of grace, agility and born genius. So good, in fact, that she had wanted the world to know it and had determined, rather bravely, that she would decree her own fate. So she had wrapped her body in her finest Tye-dyed goddessa gowns, adorned her neck, wrists and ankles with all the trinkets she'd ever made, shaved her head, painted on the virgins for luck, hoisted a basket atop her head and sojourned by foot, a great distance south, to the bustling city of Kampala. For in Uganda's capital, she would find the famous African Makkutandi Dance Troupe of Kenya...and after seeing her audition, Nuntandi knew, they would be quite and utterly *impressed.*

Not only that, but she wouldn't have to worry about the stigma of being the daughter of an Acholi tribesman. It was well known that no less than three full-blooded Acholi females were featured dancers in this most celebrated of African dance troupes and that they regularly performed in places like Europe, Italy and Sicily, Japan and the United States. Why with her talent, youth and beauty (in that order), Nuntandi realized that she would become a star instantly! So off to Uganda she ran.

On the way, she met other disobedient young girls. Some whose dreams were even bigger than hers, but unlike her, they were neither brave enough nor smart enough to be stars, Nuntandi had realized. They were mere prostitutes swarming the dirt roads and bushens like packs of well-trained but hungry dogs. With dirt-ashy black and chocolate complexions straining beneath chalky makeup that was created to flatter the out of place women (not Africans)--they called out Nuntandi's gaze with a certain wildstankpussy--scented silence. Intelligence and girl-dreams stampeding through their heads like new breeds of animals unwelcome in Africa's traditional jungle. Plenty of spit and sperm covered them, because they had no fathers, and that's what they smelled like. Hope and wishes.

*The whites of their eyes had turned canary yellow...*and the black velvet of their skin was like a carpet ripped up, oiled and dirtied, then shampooed. They reminded one of coarse purplestank goodsmoke marijuana or evil black Halloween cats or butt-ugly (*OOuh-yeah!, mom*) AIDS-infected little African whores with Eve's bad skin or the current father's bad hair. Nuntandi, in all her snobbish superiority, accepted their directions, their protection and their food. After all, it was she who would redeem them. So she behaved as a grand princess and took everything they gave--as if they were low enough to owe it.

She had no idea that almost all of these girls were *orphans....*not of the revolution. But of the *epidemic.*

"Wake up, Nuntandi...come to mama! Your baby!"

"Nun-tawndi? It's *Helen.* Helen Gator from the Women Standing Up for Women Center, hon!...why is she giggling so?"

"It's her mother's tongue she's speaking. Speaking of becoming a woman. Aii--boy magic! Ah!"

Own Me Night:

Kimba was like most of the world's men. He took pain away from the women that he cared about. He healed them. And from the moment he laid eyes on Nuntandi—he had noticed the bare-boned loneliness of her heartbroken silence. Her eyes held no illusions about courageous woman-pride or independence, she was like a newly lost scarf on the wind. Her deep eyed African beauty softly brimming with an eager submissive vulnerability that is forever to the male human what lioness urine is to the mightiest of lions. *Irresistable.*

He did not know that she had danced like a spirit fashioned of part scarf, part wind and all eternal fire on that grand stage of the African Makkutandi Dance Troupe of Kenya...or that they had applauded her wildly, cheered her ecstatically...*and then held up* beside the complexion of her glowing face--*a manila envelope,* of which Nuntandi was obviously darker, and for that reason alone--would not be allowed to join the troupe. This time, it wasn't her tribal heritage, but her black beauty that disqualified her.

It made no difference that every male dancer in the group was two buckets blacker than her or that she could out-dance all of those beautifully exotic females that were light as burnt orange clay. What mattered, the Monsignor explained to her, was that in front of rich African males and all foreigners abroad...a lighter skinned, less African-looking dancing girl was more acceptable, media-marketable and less provocative. Even on tours in the West Indies and amongst Black Americans...the cover version was preferred over the original. And out of hurt and anger, that's just how Nuntandi saw herself--as the original; the authentic black woman. The *real power.*

But Kimba had not known why she was heartbroken that first day in his uncle's garden. All he sensed was that she needed him, and being needed is a condition that men like.

He had approached her with simple caring. As if men and women could be nothing less than great comrades. That's how he courted her, each and every day, in the garden of Ghandi Mephisto.

They swirled their feet in the pond and spoke about the revolution while Nuntandi fed him flakes of tofu and slit-open roasted yams with plant's milk and ground cinnamon. She learned of his tens of thousands of brothers who had lost the war. Their reflection being his own. She learned of the nightmares that tossed him up at night. His memories going back to cutting off hands and ears, kicking in the doors of begging mothers, shooting men dead and burying children who had fallen under the might of green metal elephants. He told about poking the wives of his captured enemies, drinking swamp liquor and pissing on a portrait of Moga Davi right after helping to overthrow the bastard. He revealed to her, by telling his experiences, that he needed healing.

However, she already knew, instinctively, that Kimba's wounds were far too deep to be healed by something so pure and natural as what she felt inside herself for him. Feeling for him made her feel like a woman. Or at least she felt like what she'd been told a Basotho woman was supposed to feel like over the prospect of being chosen by a man to whom she may now shower with love, obedience and unyielding subservience. If she couldn't be of a lighter complexion or of a more powerful tribe, then she could at least be a good wife.

One day...Kimba rubbed his nose on her nose, and Ghandi Mephisto saw them and called his nephew onto the patio and rebuked him. "This girl is a servant and a runaway! Poke her in the bushes and leave her there, young lion."

The sky was a soft magenta blue that day with burning lava in the cloud slits faraway. Vultures circled an ailing brown fawn in the bush miles away. Nuntandi overheard Kimba saying, "She's a virgin, uncle. She's not stupid or common or selfish. Nuntandi is young and *willing* to be loved...and I love her. Nothing can compare to her."

In Kimba, Nuntandi knew about fire. Like a cat that leaves its master before he dies, she could smell the illness about his bones, but had not a clue that it was stronger than him. For it seemed that nothing on earth was stronger than Kimba. Nothing taller, wider, blacker or stronger. Kimba.

I love her!

Twisting the god-berry; he got the juice on his fingers.

Cheap Italian Disco Music:

Evil angels swept down from eternal white clouds, and despite all the long unmentioned love between Africans, it was the white cloud and the beauty that hides her face that slithered its cool tongue down the spine of Africa's bewildered, the three-legged, who were traditionally unkempt in the glaucoma-eyed stare of obedient wives and dark relations who historically have beat a drumbeat of false communication. *Here--line up for your injections.* With every breath, the sleeping lions fell upon their swords. Black masks reduced to white ash---a white crab munching at the follicle of pubic hair while the blood beneath dead skin itched of freedoms, seeping and ignorant, adjoining this band of angels. Like a heavy syrup, the sun poured her feminine darkness over the eyelids. Then the white men packed up their cameras, their monkeys and their legions...of flies.

Inshallah-amen.

Once a love is cast, it cannot die, but *wither* to bloom again. Each human being...being that love. For we twist the god-berry, our throats in a mighty thirst for God's juicy promise. We all, collected together as humans...are the ritual that needs to be quenched.

She needs me to love her!

Fuck that monkey-bitch in the bushes and leave her there!

This is not India, Uncle Ghandi. This is Africa. Her black-berries are needed here--she belongs!

Spoken as if...you need her...to love you.

Could we ever have ourselves to ourselves?

Africa stinks like a dying whore!

But...to wither no matter, Uncle. For she is the one thing that can grow...un-watered. Africa.

Like a field of weeds.

But if she is a weed, then she is...MY...weed. The Goddess Flower. The mother of my whole being, my own reflection--that I love more than any other. And will not cut from time's heart!

Mother Africa:

Orange fire in a trash can at early dusk as the white bottoms of charcoal black feet danced in spasms, their heels beating against the brown earth that sustained them. This is where Kimba left his mother. NunTezu. Her memory and the one before she was stoned to death.

"Return to me," she once whispered. The great mass of her lips, all the syrup inside them, kissing at the middle of his soft forehead and gently over the eyes. "Return to me."

The nipple entered his mouth and then his belly filled with milk and honey...and good African music with which to grow a lingering soul.

Or draw colored figures on flesh and mask with erect African fingers...like mothers lingering.

NunTezu had a way of staring at Kimba. A way that the other mothers did not have, because in her secrets, she knew that he was not her son, but a miracle.

The white men had handed him to her just as they handed over all their miracles:

She had been weeping profusely. Her boy had been playing with other children when a hyena leapt out of the bush and got hold of his little arm.

Dragged him dead before NunTeza could get there.

Young Kimba, just seven, had died from a bite to the skull before she could get there and cradle his head and whisper the magic words, "Return to me..

"Ten dollars for your son's body," the white scientist had said. "Ten dollars, NunTezu...and I'll bring him back to life."

Blue eyes are like windows to an impotent paradise.

So NunTezu watched the out of place men carry her dead son's limp little body back to their mysterious compound, and NunTezu's husband took the ten dollars against her wishes, and they never buried their son and NunTezu refused her husband sex--forever after.

No men, NunTezu knew, had the power to bring the dead back to life. Only our wombs, she thought, has that power. So again she had whispered, "Return to me."

And then four years later--she saw a little black baby playing in the compound's yard. It was her son! Only he was a little baby again! In the yard of the White scientists.

Born all over again! Living again! The baby even caught NunTezu staring at him, but didn't seem to recognize her. With a wobbling head, large curious eyes and a drooling mouth, he just stared out to his original mother. Seeing her.

NunTezu could not believe it. The white men had brought her dead son back into his body, starting all over from the beginning, alive again!

Her reaction was to steal the boy and run as far away to another country as she could get.

And that's just what she did.

"No, not Edward. That's not your name. Your name is Kimba. Say eeet...Keeeem-bah!"

"My name...Kimba! Kimba my name."

Like a great, beloved egbo tree, he grew tall and black right before her wet sparkling eyes. Until he was taller than. Until the smile in his mother's very black pretty face seemed as sacred as the half-moon in a purple-black jungle sky.

Until the revolution came and they were hungry and looked down upon, because NunTezu was a single mother (which is freakish), a foreigner, and she stole food to feed them...for which she was stoned to death.

Lonely man-hungry thief!

She should have gone back to her own tribe!

"When I saw Nuntandi's face and her bare breasts and the way that her head was smoothly shaven and beaded just like a princess--her eyes looked up at me--and in their lonely darkness I heard '*return to me'*...and I did not...look away."

"He is Kimba who loves me."

"I never tire...to watch her dance. For me, she laughs."

Kimba and Nuntandi:

The baby's fingertips were tiny as boiled rice pods and the face would have been Kimba's exact, thought Nuntandi. She wasn't surprised that he came out dead. Covered in an orange goo, skin like rubber, stinking. Born dead.

"I want," said Nuntandi as she began to cry, "...to die, too. This is not of a natural world. Not out of the love we made...this shouldn't be the result. We gave only purest love."

Helen Gator nodded sorrowfully after it was translated.

"Don't worry," Helen said through her own tears. "We'll find a happy ending for you." White-like like that.

And then two days later...Nuntandi was released from jail and quickly diagnosed with AIDS.

To which she responded, "I am not afraid."

"Tell her that...that I have bad news about Kimba. He's not coming back for her." The lady translated.

"No," said Nuntandi calmly. "He's waiting for me. I can *feel* it. Kimba who loves me."

"He died shortly after he left you at his uncle's compound, Nuntandi. From AIDS."

"No," she whispered through a cracking voice as her face creased with devastation, at last. Defeat bracing her dwindling frame. Her eyes virtual whirlpools of tears. She moaned out like a wounded animal, wretchedly, "...Kimba who loves me!"

I'm In the World:

Each weekend, Helen Gator donned her widest straw hat and went to the makeshift AIDS camp; rickety shanties of the Cowrie plains where the sick and dying could rest safely without danger of being beaten in the streets, thrown into rivers or set on fire by embarrassed family members. This was where Nuntandi turned eighteen one humid afternoon. Her face of black velvet and deep eyed African beauty wasted away until it was so small and shrunken that it could literally fit into the cusped hands of a child. Out of kindness, someone had preserved her African dignity and femininity by shaving her head and decorating it with the images of the river ancestors. Helen Gator, the out of place woman; the white man's mother, *kissed* her on the forehead each time she came. "Happy birthday, Nuntandi."

Someone translated for Nuntandi. Then they told Helen about the white men scheduled to arrive that day. Reporters with television cameras from America. "To show how sick and pathetic we are. The camp warden here is lining up the bleakest, blackest, ugliest of the wasting and all the children, like legions of flies--so their disease can be photographed first."

"They never show our grand cities," snorted a rather healthy woman; one of the nurses. "They never show us in church or in our seats at university. They never show our elaborate wedding ceremonies or the fathers teaching the boys to hunt, the mothers teaching the girls to weave. They never show the contest between the homes--to see who has the oldest warrior mask on the wall. Our great legacy of un-killable Kings and Queens, our great civilizations. No, no, white lady. They come to show our death. As much as they can film it. To make us so pitiful and lowly that our children won't want to be like *us* anymore. They want to show themselves, their white hands, giving us food and medicine. Their bloody white hands. They want to show that we are the pollution of the world--when it's really *your people* who are. They want to make our children ashamed of us and hate Africa. Want to be white or be like the niggers you created. And return no more. But every night, my husband tells our son...'*return* to me!"

Helen didn't know what to say. She simply nodded politely and took a seat next to Nuntandi's cot. She was glad to see the huge smile on the girl's tiny face as she handed her several birthday gifts--a new pillow, a new bowl, *baby powder!,* a beaded necklace from the village craftswomen.

"You are...a very kind white lady."

"It's nothing at all between sisters," Helen said holding Nuntandi's hand. "I'm just so sorry that you were stuck in that horrible jail for so long. I consider it my fault."

"But white lady. Nuntandi says in her language...'It's O.K. I've been in prison all my life'."

"Oh really? Where at?"

"Nuntandi say...'*wherever I was'.*"

Signature of the Illicit:

"Soon," said Helen. "I must return to America. There is an election going on and I must help Bill Clinton defeat George Bush. I will be gone at least six months, Nuntandi."

The translator deliberately kept this from Nuntandi. She told the girl something else and then translated the reply. Helen removed her crucifix necklace and offered it as a goodbye, but Nuntandi refused it. Waved the thing away.

Nuntandi spoke, her eyes watching God.

"Sometimes I am so happy. When my eyes are *closed...*I begin to dance and I'm in the world. I'm in the world. I have my admirers watching on and Kimba has returned to me. And my baby not dead. He a boy. Boy magic. Alive and well and calling for me to come put him on my back and take him across the river. Like all the mothers before me. So he can be a man one day. Like his father. Like my father. Like *your* father. Sometimes, I am so happy. So happy that all I can do is dance, because this is happiness to me, to dance."

"You know...the television crew has asked the warden for permission to interview you on camera. One of the producers walked by and noticed how you are always smiling. This will make you a big star in America!" cheered Helen. Her hands were clasped together beneath her chin, her pearly white teeth glistening. So here she was...out of place and strangely naive. The white man's mother.

To which a stunned and diminishing Nuntandi quietly advised: "If you truly believe in God, then be careful not to brag--for if God observes that you are strong enough to take a bullet--then surely, he will arrange for you to be shot. That is the way of all Gods...Hell-in. I don't do *interviews.*"

Day of Vow

She stuck with it...being a glassmaker. When you make glass, there's an experience as it forms when the matter is so fiery liquid and lava-taffy hot, becoming more and more of itself like the ocean that it is literally intoxicating and otherworldly hypnotic. Like something from Mars or hell or inside the sun. Beautiful as anything you could dream about paralyzed. That's how it felt having the privilege and the blessed luck to make glass for a living.

It wasn't a normal job for a South African woman, educated or otherwise to occupy...but Zorina had been doing it since she was eight (the house maid's curious little daughter back then), and now at seventeen, no one at the furnace could match her craftsmanship. The Theron family was making quite a name (not to mention a pretty penny) for itself because of this quaint little wonder, and Zorina, too, had an obsessive interest in their manor born. Miss Lindy and sweet little Cribbitch could absolutely send one.

But the person who really intrigued her, even more than glass, was the Theron family son--nineteen year old polo champion Noble Theron--who had raped Zorina when she was thirteen. The Therons called him "Golf." He was tall and handsome, chilly white with an innocent soldier boy's face and warm glacier-blue eyes. He fascinated Zorina to no end, mainly because he had lived for a while in what she considered to be life's promised land--America; and then, too, because he had raped her and then seemingly forgotten all about it (as if she had just imagined the whole thing)--and this only increased Zorina's pain until all she could do was pass out from it (have a nervous breakdown) or become fascinated by the source of that pain.

"Haven't I told you not to call me Golf when we're alone, Zora?"

"Yes, Noble," she always replied with as feminine an incantation as possible.

At the mere sight of him, Zorina always felt dizzy in the tummy and weak in the knees. Like most white men in South Africa, Golf moved about like a stern wire coat hanger.

"And do sit down, girl. I want your delightful company more than any breakfast. You know that."

On the veranda's cool dawn, the sun barely up and cloud white butterflies fluttering about the garden, Golf Theron took his milk with a spoonful of cognac and his oatmeal with cream and sugar. They sat together; two extremely secretive people. Zorina more than him--because only she knew about the little match box that she kept in her skirt's front pocket and the tiny black pellets inside (rat turds). Only she knew how metallic and perfectly formed they looked, like little black rice pods, as she took a few out each morning and stirred them into his oatmeal right after her mother cooked it up. And every morning, for years, he had eaten it all down, and that's what helped Zorina justify her love for him. She thought that he must be as poisoned and tricked inside as she was by now. Her being raped at Theron Estate and violently burned at school and his stomach full of rat turds made them seem perfect for each other.

"So you've heard about the tennis match?" he asked Zorina.

Her face, a lemony ice-tea color, was instantly lit with a grin. Like all the other South African black girls, she had cheered the arrival of Venus and Serena Williams (Americans!) and had been overjoyed to see an African-*looking* girl play tennis and beat the turd out of Amanda Coetzer, South Africa's white champ. All over the country, in the streets and- dirt roads, the blacks had cheered and rooted: "Go Venus! Go Venus!"As if *Venus* was the South African. So yes, Zorina had heard. Her mother had even made a keg of beer for the ghetto's celebration and black fathers had danced bare chested in the streets with *VENUS* written across their hearts in the bloodiest red paint they could find.

Golf Theron blushed and gave a cave-dark grin. He whispered across the table, "I was rooting for Venus, too."

Heat covered Zorina's forehead. Like it did every morning when Golf was done with breakfast. Because that's when he always rose, towering over her...and swaggered on by, deliberately brushing his athletic hairy leg against her lean brown arm. For a split second, she remembered his weapon of authority; erect--the only manpart she had ever known. His mighty white skin touched her clean brown embarrassment. His white tennis shorts, the ones that Zorina's mother washed and ironed in stacks each week, seemed so fresh and pure; so sunshine bright and snow white.

Whiter even--than the sickle shaped burn seared into Zorina's right buttock like a pothole of saintly white ashes.

"Carry on, Zora."

In a breathy voice.

"Yes...Noble."

But once he was gone and her mother had cleared away the dishes he left behind, Zorina always managed to turn back into herself. Humming some American pop song (*"I Can't Tell You Why"* by the Eagles) as she left the veranda and passed Miss Lindy's gazebo, the swing set for Cribbitch, the heavenly green arc of field and forest that shaded the horse stables...and finally, on down the dirt road past the creek, her favorite place in the whole world...the Theron furnace.

Three brick chimneys pointed up from the old building like a crown and the trees on either side of it seemed ageless and ancient--brittle gray and undying. Zorina's mother always told her that "trees are loyal beings." The furnace house was made of granite with a cobblestone floor inside the entrance hall. On the hook outside, she always hung her sweater before placing a sak lunch in the little locker that made her feel accomplished and important, because it had her name written across it in typed ink. Golf Theron had done that.

Ebaneezer called out, "That you, Milady!?"

"Yes it is!" Zorina hollared back with a grin.

He was having breakfast in the nook. His face pink like strawberry ice cream and his chin and cheeks always foaming witha white unkempt beard. He was a fat, stinking soot-covered Santa Klaus-looking man with ale on his breath and gas passing from his arse every twenty minutes...but he had a heart of gold.

Zorina entered the nook. "Balu inside already?"

Ebaneezer nodded and farted.

Balu was the new glassmaker from Cape Town. He was Indian and had a wife who was half-black, half-Korean...and since the two of them were legally coloured (which is a *higher class* than plain old black in South Africa), they didn't allow their two children to play with black, kinky-headed kaffir kids.

Balu had told this information to Golf Theron (to affirm, as coloured South Africans do, his loyalty to whiter sensibilities) and then Golf had turned into Noble and told Zorina. So Zorina didn't like Balu--because she knew a lot of Indians, Asians and mixed race people that were like that. In fact, according to her dead father, Africa was infested with them.

The other glassmaker on the premises, Othello, he was mixed-race, but he wasn't like that at all. For whenever whites called a black person "kaffir"--it was as if they had called

Othello himself that horrible word. He considered himself an African and would say it out loud to anybody's face. His wife, however, was as ugly as raw liver according to Zorina's mother. He could've had his pick instead of choosing a girl who was so darkskinned and walked and talked with the smell of sex in her personality. Him being such an eggcreme pretty fellow with a good job and so ruggedly mannish with those big soccer legs and that curly Italic hair (his father was Italian-Lebanese and his mother was a black South African woman, herself part Indian). Wasting himself on some low class chocolate kaffir bitch, Zorina's mother would say. Here he was now.

"Greetings, Zorina!"

"Hey...top of the morning, Othello! How's LissaMondi?"

"Oh, mighty good going. The baby kicked this morning and Lissa graduates from nursing school next saturday. I'm inviting everyone for stew and bread. You bring your Brenda Fassie albums, Zorina!"

"I'll have to sneak them past Big Mama," she laughed.

**

The flames resemble pieces of hellfire tumbling around like clothes in a washing machine. Capable of baking the face six shades if one doesn't wear a protective mask. It's hot like an oven down there. The sweating is unavoidable and yet the skin beneath the sweat remains dry, parched and crackly. The blistered smell of the liquid glass as it's looped and spun, twirled or blown...transformed from recipe to imagination to creation's beauty both challenges and resists Zorina every time, but her standard of taste is not a will be stilled.

"Hers are special," Balu whispered enviously whenever she set a sea-crystal wine goblet atop the cooling board.

"She's gifted," snorted Ebaneezer, as if Balu had better recognize that he is not the big maestro he thought he was back in Cape Town. He's just a talented backup singer now.

"Damn, that's pretty," said Othello as he glanced at the intricate spheres, the way the light was alive beneath the precise layers of Zorina's spooling sheath. He got a lump in his throat just looking at it. Her creations looked more like jewelry than table wear.

"It's all in the wrist," bragged the little brown girl.

"No, no...the heart," smiled Othello, tenderly.

**

In the late evening when Zorina and her mother took the state worker's bus from the back road of the Theron Estate all the way to the dirt roads of the ghetto shanties of Sowego, the transition felt as normal to them as breathing. They were slightly higher class than most of their neighbors, because being the head maid for a family as rich and well known as Dutch Theron's was a major coup, and more than that, Zorina's status as glassmaker provided her the rank of a college graduate and surpassed all the menial factory jobs that the local men were allowed to hold. She and her mother were looked up to.

"I need time for the wedding dress," Etah, Zorina's mother, sighed, as the two of them busied themselves setting supper in the small of their kitchen. "The hours inside the night just aren't deep enough."

Zorina, solemn and deeply breathing, tried not to burst into tears.

Etah was a hefty woman with a profound pair of buttocks and huge feet like a camel's. In the center of her face she was pretty. She greatly resembled the beautiful American actress

Alfre Woodard, her spitting image, only Etah was fat and had much lighter skin. She wore a rag around her head and sometimes grimaced from the arthritis plaguing her knees and left shoulder. Her man had been dead for years, so her thinking skills weren't as whiplash quick as they had once been. Mainly, she let herself settle into acting a lot older than she actually was and looking like, too.

"Oh...I've got to sit down."

"Big Mama, get off your feet now."

Zorina had the pot of red beans, rice and oxtails heating up (leftovers), and Etah would just have to make herself a little pan of peppercorn broth to go over the bread. Her late husband had always loved having his peppercorn broth over some bread.

"I've got to work some with that dress," restated Etah, and Zorina's heart jumped again at the mention of it. She could just imagine all the lavish white lace, satin, tulle...flowing beneath the soft pretty whiteness of Maritza Buitengracht--the proper young lady who was engaged to marry Golf Theron in just another month.

"Let her buy a dress in Durban, Mama. They'll shop and horse race this coming weekend as it is."

"Miss Lindy wants Maritza to wear the same dress that she wore. It needs lots of alterations, because that Maritza girl is no bigger than a strand of straw. Skinnier than you, Zorina, if that's possible."

"You think Golf really loves her, Mama?"

"I think he's like any other man entering marriage--he'll act out what he's seen others do. But it's Miss Lindy that picked her. Brought her back from Europe and set it up. She sure is a lovely girl, I'll say. Just as beautiful as a snow white princess from a land of angels."

Instantly, Zorina recalled the time that she and a friend had been in line at the cinema house and overheard a group of handsome black boys repeating a saying that's very popular among South African black men. Two boys told another boy: "White women don't need to take baths, because God made them clean by nature and they never smell."

Zorina blacked out just thinking about Maritza's long, golden tresses of angel's hair and the gorgeous way it flowed heavily down her back like wavy yellow sunshine. She floated away thinking about how Golf always held that dainty little white hand and kissed it just so...like it belonged to a Queen.

"I hate Golf Theron," Zorina heard herself say. Her voice tight and mean. It surprised and startled Etah.

"But what, my daughter?"

"I said I hate Golf Theron, mama. He doesn't deserve a beautiful white woman like Maritza Buitengracht, she's too good for him, mama."

Etah rallied back with her maid-like instincts. She insisted, "But Golf has *always* been a good boy! He's as handsome and kindhearted as a man could come, Zorina!"

Zorina almost mouthed off and reminded her mother of the time that Golf had told classmates visiting from his boarding school that Etah was part of an ancient ape tribe and then asked her, right in front of all those white giggling faces, to speak "planet of the apes language." But Zorina said nothing.

Teardrops, huge and wet began swelling and falling into an emotional breakdown as Zorina screamed out, "If I could rip out his throat, I'd do it! With my bare hands, I'd do it!"

"*What!?*"

Etah was no dummy. She'd seen that kind of bitterness in the eyes of black worker-bee women before, but she couldn't risk hearing what might come out of her daughter's mouth next. For if it came out to be rape, then Etah might have to do something about it, and courage had never been Etah's strongsuit. So instead, she jumped to her feet and slapped the living shit out of her daughter!

"SHUT... UP!"

The shock of it stunned Zorina to complete stillness, her eyes bulging and her back tense as though a pan of cold water had been dumped over her head. "Now you stop this jealousy you have towards white girls and thank our sweet lord for the privileges that you do have, you selfish black arse! I won't have you say another bad word against Mister Theron. He's a good boy, educated and handsome and he treats you like you're his own sister, Zorina! You don't know how spoiled you are by the Therons, that's the problem! He lets you call him *Noble,* and not even his own mother calls him that! What's that? You thought I didn't know your little secret?"

An iceberg moved between them.

"Alright then, mama," whispered Zorina. "I...*love* Noble."

Then she left her supper on the table and went up to bed.

In the dim light of her bedroom, fully unaffected by the sound of mice playing in the walls, Zorina stood naked in the half mirror staring at herself. She couldn't imagine how anyone could think for a single moment that Maritza Buitengracht was more beautiful than she was. Obviously, Noble knew the truth. He was the one who always insisted that Zorina looked exactly like the gorgeous movie actress Thandie Newton (only Zorina was four shades browner)...and wasn't it *Zorina's hair* that had fascinated Noble when she was just a child? Hadn't he marveled at how soft it was--natural, springy African hair worn in a medium afro? Hadn't Golf liked putting his hands in it often (without permission as white people do)?

From Golf, Zorina had learned that nothing gets dirty faster than *white* skin. Or can smell more foul. So black men in

South Africa certainly didn't know what they were talking about.

Carefully, just as she did every night, she applied several coats of pure vitamin E oil to the burn on her bottom.

Zorina thought this whole entire world must be insane to think that Golf could find a better woman than her. But then again, white men were different from other men Zorina had observed. White men admired themselves and their race far too much not to give birth to purely white children. That was the catch, Zorina realized. It was their own white children that they loved so dearly, more than life itself, and for that, she couldn't help but respect them.

Zorina pulled the covers over her head and drifted off to sleep.

Once asleep, she was back at Children of Christ Protectorate School. Eve was holding her hand. She could see the charred black door again...lava red beneath the blackened wood. The only classroom was burnt down around it, smoke everywhere. Most of the children beneath the rubble were burnt to a white crisp. It was a black school (without whites or coloureds), so the fire brigade didn't arrive until the next day. But Zorina had escaped with her life.

She had lived to see the newspaper headlines that blamed the fire on radical white men protesting Mandela's *new* South Africa, and within hours, the entire world was outraged to learn that white men had burned up forty-two innocent little black children. Riots broke out...for three days straight.

Riots.

But Zorina and Eve looked at each other now.

They knew that it wasn't white men who had deliberately burned those children to death, the teachers, too.

Etah laid in bed like a whale and cried like a baby. Above her head hung the portrait of Queen Elizabeth II that her husband had proudly nailed to the wall on the very first day that they had moved into the house. In fact, after carrying Etah over the threshold, the portrait had been the first item of decoration that he'd carried into the house, even before a single piece of furniture. His mother had cherished it all her life and given it to the young couple as a life's luck gift. She bid her son to respect it as if it were she herself. So Nopopie had adored the portrait of Queen Elizabeth II, and now by laying beneath it at night, Etah felt that she was especially close to her late husband's spirit. She believed that through Elizabeth II, Nopopie could hear her more clearly.

"Nopopie...it is me, again. *Etah,*" she cried. "I feel as if none of our children have understood the warning in your murder, dear husband. The way those white devils kicked holes in your stomach and left you in the church restroom to die. Like you were just trash, dear husband."

The police had claimed Nopopie assaulted one of them after they had politely asked to see his traveling permit.

"I worry about Zorina," she wailed, tearfully. "I fear she's been compromised, like your mother and sister were when you were just a boy and couldn't protect them."

His smell came into the room, because Etah missed him.

She missed the way he said grace at mealtime.

She missed the times when he drank and cursed the white overseers who worked him mercilously at the mines, making him beg every week for that pitifully low paying job, and then talked down to him like he was a boy.

She missed the times, right after Nopopie had brutally beaten her (clocked her upside the head with his boot)...the times afterward when he would pull her long, wide skirt up over her head and plunge his manhood deep inside her. She ached for the banging and the wretched sobbing--of a man sincerely sorry about the cruel ways in which he abused and humiliated her.

"I love you, my Etah!"

"I know you do, Nopopie. I know you do," she used to cry, so patiently, as her eyes were swollen shut and blood ran from her nose and busted lip.

Other times, he would beat her up and then take out his manhood and urinate right in her face. All in her hair and down her pregnant belly. "I can't afford all these kids, bitch!"

But she missed him now so much that she'd gladly go through it all again. Every moment of hurt and humiliation. Just to see him, touch him and know again...that he loved her.

Etah got up and put on some music. Miriam Makeba, Etta James, Burning Spear. She took her headrag off and greased the thick, soft African bushhead. Hot tea was sipped down. Prayers to Jesus Christ were hummed, spoken and cried passionately. She promised herself that she would clean up Miss Lindy's massage room real good tomorrow and get that blasted dress worked on.

Then she slept...and snored tremendously.

Eve's Monkey had been missing ever since the fire.

Zorina bolted upright in bed!

Awake.

Breathing hard.

Wondering if it were Eve and Jesus Christ again--outside her window, standing barefoot on the dirt road--calling her.

She wished it were...but it wasn't.

She wished Winnie Mandela was her mother, but she wasn't.

She wished everyone knew that Golf Theron just couldn't get her out of his mind, but she was a kaffir girl, and therefore, no one would *ever* believe it.

She wished her classmates hadn't screamed so horribly as their flesh burned, their bones crackled like firewood and their lungs strained, coughing.

She could still hear them.

She could still hear every last one of them.

Crying out wretchedly for their mamas.

**

Before dawn, Zorina and her mother were back at the Theron Estate. Preparing the house for when everyone awakened. At daybreak, Golf arose to have his usual oatmeal with his usual rat turds while Zorina sat by waiting to be brushed up against before a long, satisfying tournament of glassmaking.

It had been nine years since the school burned down, but as Zorina was experiencing cramps that morning and the start of her monthly bleeding, it didn't seem so long ago, because along with her monthlies always came a nagging pain in the scar tissue of her burn. As though the burn were new again.

"What's in that pretty little head, ha?" asked Golf. "Keeping secrets are we?"

"No..Noble."

In the beautiful oceans of his blue eyes she thought that she wanted to backstroke naked. Feel the beating of his heart against her warm golden body. Be swept away.

Suddenly, Etah appeared--filling up the back door in her giant maid's uniform. She had none of Hattie McDaniel's famous sass.No subdued outrage like the American star had shown in all her gallant portrayals of black maid women. Etah was a *real* servant spirit. "My daughter?"

"Oh!...ahhh...yes, mama!?"

"Miss Lindy would like to see you in the library."

"Is that my Zorina!?"

"Top of the morning, Miss Lindy."

"You've got to get packed dear. We're flying to Durban."

"...ew...wu...*Durban*?"

Cribbitch, her sweet blonde crystal-blue eyed little daughter chimed in with: "Mummy's having a glass show at the Wedgwood Gallery."

"Your glassworks are making me famous, Zorina!"

"But, I haven't anything to wear."

"It's alright, love. No one expects a black to be dressed that well, but I want you to represent the furnace workers."

Miss Lindy, who led people to believe that she actually designed and self-crafted the Dutch Theron Glass Collection, hadn't been inside the ahouse for twelve years. Her husband, Dutch, had a reputation for taking his Indian whores down there at night, so Miss Lindy refused to set her wifely heels on those sticky floors.

"Oh, Zorina! They're giving me an *award!*"

"Glassmaker of the year," chirped Cribbitch.

It never occured to any of them (not even Zorina) that the award should be given to Zorina.

"Hurry home and pack," cheered Cribbitch. "We've already told Etah that you're going away."

**

Zorina tried to remember how the poem went. *I come from a place...*

As the plane lifted out of Johannesburgh and creased blue sky towards Durban, Zorina tried to remember how the poem went:

I come from a place...but my place is not named for me

I am the caretaker, unnamed,

the insider

whose heartbeat you hear.

I have no place...not even my own

footprints

have any place.

She had never seen how breathtakingly beautiful South Africa is from the sky. How earthen brown and green and soulful the landscape is. An African's dream; kissed by God.

"My place" Zorina thought...as tears ran down her dark cheek and she thought of her devoted mother, her dead father. *Mines!*

One day, she prayed, all the whites would be gone from South Africa. So that the black people could take the time necessary to get over all the cruel and inhumane evils that the Europeans had so lavishly carried out. Even in the name of God, they had carried out unspeakable evils that could never *really* be forgtten. It seemed so unfair, their being here...living high and mighty off the backs and the land of Africa's true children.

Zorina wondered how it felt to die by having community police kick holes in your stomach? And knowing how many black men and black women had experienced such horrifying deaths in South Africa, she wondered how many *whites* had experienced such evil?

"Remove them, God."

Zorina put her head back and stared out the window to the gliding wing of the plane (she was seated alone). That's when Eve's face popped into her memory. Little girl Eve. So charcoal black that she wasn't allowed to be registered at Children of Christ Protectorate School...even though it was founded, funded and ran by two black men. Eve's charcoal coloring prevented her from attending, and two decades before that, Eve's mother, one of several dozen *charcoal* prostitutes, had been deterred from seeking education due to the same skin problem.

The secret came back to Zorina now.

"It's morning time!" one of the black Reverends had said when Eve's Monkey tried to register.

These two Bantu clergymen, schoolteachers, were of South Africa's popular belief that the black race was moving away from oppression and the *darkness* that caused that oppression. Girls like Eve were a threat, because no one wanted those genes passed on.

Little charcoal black "*boys*"(in fact, one of them was Eve's very own brother) were allowed to attend classes. But whenever a charcoal black girl tried to register--the men did not allow it. Why even the two girls as chocolate as mud were allowed in--but not girls as charcoal black as Eve's Monkey.

"Don't call me Eve's Monkey!" the seven year old barefoot girl had hissed back at one of the clergymen one day. "That's not my name!" the girl had cried.

"Well, you look like a monkey!" retorted the Reverend. A grown man, a chocolate-skinned man, a man of the cloth. "And you won't be enrolled here, you smelly, ugly little oil stain! It's morning time!"

Everyday, Zorina had witnessed it. The little blue black girl marching barefoot, dressed in rags to the school building. All the other girls her color had accepted their rejection on notice, but not this nervy little black thing. She was brave!

"I want to learn to read and count my fingers!" Eve's Monkey would beg.

"Go to monkey and ape school, little prostitute!"

Brilliant laughter.

Zorina could see all the children now. Little chocolates, milky browns, golden browns, light browns, yellows, *blue black "boys"*--and especially Sowego's majority color (peanut butter browns)...oh they had a belly laugh! Little girls with Afros, pigtails and some with long, thick black perms--they shot their shining brown eyes at Eve with venomous disgust.

"You're too ignorant to learn!' shouted Eve's own brother. "You're so ugly, the school books won't stay in your hands!"

"They left you in the oven too long!" shouted one fat yam yellow girl.

"Why doesn't she grow some hair!?"

Zorina could feel it again now...*the heat* and the pain and how everyone was suddenly in flames and the roof caved in and lucky for Zorina, she was away from her desk sharpening her pencil by the only door that led outside. She had braced her nose against the gasoline fumes as she ran out...and she had spotted Eve running through the green pastures barefoot, dressed in rags, laughing.

She had watched Eve running, in fact, until Eve evaporated into the hillside...like a ghost. Then other dead children, children whose bodies were still burning inside the school, they began following Eve into the hillside...as if they were all going away to play together...and that was when Zorina fell in love with the fires that shape glass. Their spirits had all looked like clear glass objects to Zorina, joyfully leaping into a careless paradise. Zorina had wanted to go! Everyone else was going! But one of the dead boys yelled, "You stay here!"

Zorina was just eight then...and no one thought to put her into therapy for what she had experienced, and of course, the tragedy would be blamed on white men's racism, not black men's racism, but Zorina couldn't have cared less if white men were held responsible for it.

The hotel in Durban was exquisite.

Unfortunately, Zorina's traveling with Miss Lindy and Cribbitch always meant that she would act as surrogate maid and secretary. She had to unpack and hang up their clothes properly, prepare their baths and fix their meals, because Miss Lindy always reserved a suite with its own well stocked kitchen.

She couldn't even tell them that she was bleeding. That's how genuinely close they were.

Meanwhile, down the street, cases of the glass pieces, almost every one of them conceived and crafted on the spot by Zorina, were pulled out of padded boxes by specially trained handlers and aligned along the gallery walls. Lindy Theron was there to marvel at the wonders that bore her husband's good name. She couldn't wait for the awards presentation dinner!

"We should get a dress, mummy," said Cribbitch suddenly. "A dress for Zorina to wear. It's her big night, too. She hasn't anything to wear and she's so pretty, mum."

"I guess I could do that much," nodded Lindy. "I don't want her standing behind me in the photographs looking like some unfed prairie dog."

Back at the hotel, Zorina sat suddenly on one of the beds she was custom making. She was dizzy and bleeding and felt like she was dying. Her cramps were like stomach punches!

She lay down on the bed...flat...and stared up at the ceiling.

Out of nowhere, she began to miss her mother, intensely, as if she might not ever see the plump, pretty face again. Zorina had always been a girl who knew instinctively that *mothers need their daughters.*

And she loved Etah more than anyone in this world.

"O...", gasped Cribbitch. "That is so pretty on you!"

Zorina couldn't believe she was being fitted in such a gown as the one Cribbitch had picked for her. Cribbitch might only be twelve, but she was a very sophisticated little girl and her taste in clothes was impeccable.

Shiny, lemon-tea light brown with the loveliest face and a perfect crown of cottony African bush hair on her head, Zorina looked like a Zulu princess in a strapless, flowing white Athenian tube gown complete with golden arm bracelets and gold bangles. The dinner was being given outdoors by fire pit (with a roasted pig and dancing Zulu girls), so it was only fitting that Zorina be dressed summer-like and glamorous. At just seventeen years old, she was too stunning for words.

"The only thing I don't like," said Miss Lindy, "is the way the..."

Zorina already knew what it was. She had feared it, too.

"...well, your bottom fits the dress funny."

Zorina's heart sank, because it was her big butt that was always messing up the shape of her clothes, and she was too skinny, way too thin to be cursed already with her mother's big fat firm, heartshaped ass. She burst into tears!

"Oh, Zorina...no, honey. Don't cry."

Zorina collapsed into Miss Lindy's arms. Her heart full with memories of the way her father had always teased her mother's backside by calling it "*funk-trunk*". It was such an ugly name, a cruel endearment. Etah had always hated it and yet Nopopie would go on and on about the *sweat* collecting between the crack...of Etah's funk-trunk.

"Now you listen to me...you look like a fashion model in that dress! Naomi Campbell would be proud! And as far as you being able to afford it...well, we'll just take a percentage from your salary every other week until it's paid for."

Zorina sobered up immediately. She wanted to say: *Why don't we just pawn that award you're getting and pay for the dress--you selfish caucasoid bitch!* But, of course, she didn't dare say it.

Thank God Cribbitch said it!

"Mummy!...Zorina's already earned that dress! She's the one who made all this beautiful glass that you're getting an award for. She shouldn't have to pay for that gown--rich as you and daddy are!"

Miss Lindy turned pink and relented.

But on the way back to the hotel, all Zorina could think about was the way that the black boys in her neighborhood were always dreaming of being rappers or athletes and how a girl like herself might be walking by and they might go: "Funk-trunk pussy stain...bang, bang, bang.....Funk-trunk pussy stain ...bang, bang, bang."

It was supposed to be a compliment. It was supposed to mean that she was sexually desirable. However, Zorina was smart enough to know the difference between a boy dreaming about banging up inside a hot-hole and a boy dreaming about *making love* to a girl. These boys, so dark and handsome, imagined her as nothing more than meat for sex.

Zorina figured that some unseen mystery girl, probably not from Sowego, was their choice for dreams about lovemaking, but whatever the case, she foolishly blamed her *funk-trunk* for her status with neighborhood boys.

The next night...Golf Theron arrived in Durban!

With his beautiful fiance, Maritza.

"I wouldn't miss your big night for the world, mother!"

Miss Lindy grinned, proudly, and kissed him and hugged him. "Oh, my baby boy!"

Zorina was dizzy with excitement--because Golf was going to get to see her all dressed up in her glamorous evening wear! It was just too good to be true!

But first...she was told to custom make Golf and Maritza's separate beds. So she went to their suite. First, she went into Golf's room and made his bed. Then she went to Maritza's room. There was music coming from the dressing room that led to the bathroom. It was Diana Ross singing, *"It's My House and I Live Here."* For some reason, hearing that song in Maritza's bathroom made Zorina intensely jealous. She didn't think that Diana Ross should be christening Maritza's territory.

She heard faint laughter.

Obviously, Golf was in the dressing room with Maritza.

Zorina could smell him. His cologne. Then suddenly they laughed out really loud, Golf's voice proclaiming from behind the wall, "I must be in love with an angel!"

*I am an angel...*Zorina wanted to proclaim out loud, as tears moistened her large brown eyes, not so much for Golf, but for the God who had cast her black and African.

Zorina couldn't help herself.

Really, she couldn't.

She went to the crack in the doorway of the dressing room and peeped inside.

Beautiful gowns, jewels...strewn everywhere.

Apparently, Maritza was trying on different outfits and Golf was there to lust over the creamy white contours of her incredibly tiny body. Her breasts, thought Zorina, were like slivers of liver hanging with big, cherry nipples. But her hair was incredible--flowing like gold all around her shoulders. Her face was so pale, like the Queen Elizabeth II portrait over Etah's bed. Pale like a queen.

"Is there anything I could want more than an angel?"

"Yes, a woman," replied Maritza.

Golf chuckled at her sharpness, and there was a way that he held her. Held her in his arms like she was grace itself. It was so incredibly endearing to Zorina's watching eyes. A kind of poetry in motion that she suddenly remembered dreaming about...wide awake sometimes, asleep other times. Now she remembered that she had dreamed about that kind of silly, emotional hanging on. Like in cinema films.

No. It was better than that. This couldn't be staged.

The way his eyes searched for Maritza in the mirror even though she was right up against him.

He loved her hair--he fingered around in it.

His chin rested on her shoulder and Zorina knew, intuitively, that they had never ever made love and that Maritza was a virgin. She just knew it.

"You smell like sunshine," he told Maritza.

"It's called *Privilege* by Dutchess Wayborn."

His hands fastened in front of her and his dreamy blue eyes closed and rocked her gently.

At the door, Zorina slid slowly, quietly, to the floor. There were no tears in her eyes now. She was totally engrossed in watching Golf behave just as she had dreamed he would.

"How many children should we have?"

"Two," she said. "A boy and a girl."

"Only two?" he growled.

Then he tickled her. She giggled and shook free of him.

Zorina noticed that they had the prettiest wine she had ever seen--sitting in glasses in front of the mirror. What beautiful color! What richness! It had to be absolutely delicious, Zorina thought, and her tastebuds suddenly went to fantasizing about what it must taste like. A wine that red and pretty. *I...made those glasses,* she suddenly realized.

Golf lifted a glass just then and took a swig from it. His white knuckles against the stem. Zorina's nipples hardened...her heart panted and her eyes felt as though someone had suddenly blown hard in them.

He put the rim of the glass to Maritza's thin rosy lips and she drank a swallow, comfortably closing her eyes and sinking back into the warmth of his chest.

"You make me so happy, Golf."

"I told you not to call me Golf when we're alone. Call me Noble."

She giggled and said, "Yes...*Noble*."

Zorina suddenly couldn't see a thing.

Not through her tears.

She went about the task of custom making Maritza's bed.

Fluffing the pillows with an extra something--her admiration for Maritza. In and out of her mind, the memories of being raped by Golf Theron at thirteen sprung up like some annoying radio tune that she couldn't stop humming.

Tears fell off her chin...onto the lavish bedcovers.

Some old blues song was coming from the dressing room. A drunk lady singing out: "*...put that dog in the back-ah the house...tie 'em up; tie 'em up...hand me my pigfoot, hand me my beer!...tie 'em up; tie 'em up...*"

Zorina was done with the bed.

Just then...Golf came tumbling out of the dressing room.

He halted as Zorina turned startled and said, "...Zorina!"

She wasn't accustomed to him calling her Zorina, so she said, "It's Zora to *you*...remember?"

Golf gulped. He came over to her and said in a low voice, "I really need to talk to you about something before you go to bed this evening. It's about us, Zorina. It's really important. Could you come to my room later--around midnight?"

About us Zorina.

That was so shocking to hear out of a white man's mouth and she couldn't believe that he was acknowledging that there was an *us* between them. Honestly, she had started to believe that she was just some fool traumatized by a rape, obsessed with getting from the rapist himself some kind of acceptance or forgiveness or approval.

But he had said *us* just now.

"Will you come, please?"

"Yes...Noble."

**

Miss Lindy was all teeth, wrinkles and huge blonde hair as she went up to receive the award for Glassmaker of the Year.

The entire dinner was for her. There were no competitors, no judges, no nominees. She thanked a long list of people, but not one of them was Zorina.

Othello came.

He had driven up with his wife LissaMondi, but some old white man had turned them away at the door and by the time Miss Lindy was told of it, it was too late.

Zorina could smell the smoke from the school again, but she tried not to let it get to her. She was the only black person at the whole affair and found herself roundly ignored.

Completely and absolutely.

For one thing--her young body in the strapless, tight white gown had upstaged all of the other women. The fact that she was such a pretty girl and the *only* oasis of colored skin in the room had made her into a striking kind of exotic goddess flower. It took Zorina a few hours to figure out that white people don't appreciate it when a black woman does something that only white women are supposed to be able to do. They could accept her as a young, raggedy maid--but not as a beautiful black woman *of childbearing age*.

The biggest surprise was Golf's strange behavior.

He didn't look at Zorina one...single...time. Even when she spoke to him (to get him to look) he acted as if she were butt naked or something. The other men seemed to sweat whenever she walked by them. They clung to their wives and girlfriends as if they felt literally threatened. Zorina felt dirty, because not even the waiters and maids (all Indians and Asians) would acknowledge her presence or her beauty. Cribbitch was too young to attend the party and Maritza Buitengracht simply didn't socialize with kaffir girls in public, period.

Out of great fires, the breathtaking glasses that Zorina had created lined their velvet tiers like trophies, and increasingly, Zorina wanted to scream out that *she* was the one who had formed and sculpted every one of them by hand! It was *her* they gathered to honor--the kaffir girl! All of this glassed beauty was because of the monumental sorrow that had pushed forth her genius, but she couldn't do that to the Theron family and get away with it. The cost would be too high. Like the mice who lived in the walls back home, the white people scampered around merrily, careful not to make eye contact or place themselves in the open, away from the safety of the walls. How many souls had they nibbled on to stand here munching caviar and sipping martinis--and why did Zorina want so desperately to be acknowledged and accepted by them?

By the end of the night, Zorina felt as if she were just a coffee stain on somebody's white silk lap napkin.

**

She made it to Golf and Maritza's suite at two in the morning. Golf, who seemed to have been waiting by the door, let her in and then quickly rushed her through the black darkness to the lighted doorway of his room. It had been years since his hands had gripped Zorina's body this way and she thought she might pee on herself from the adrenaline that was pulsing through her veins as his large white hands tightened around her soft little cinnamon-stick arm.

"Don't make a sound," he whispered harshly, his breath smelling like liverwurst and scotch, and there was no more music, no more light coming from Maritza's room. Just black silence--her door closed.

Slowly, Golf closed the door to his own room and Zorina wondered how she should act? She had seen Halle Berry in a cinema film and liked the combination of vulnerability and strength that the actress possessed. She thought she could act like that and stand her ground no matter what he said. She might even get loud if he said the wrong thing...so that people would wonder what a little kaffir girl had been doing in the privacy of his room at such an ungodly hour.

But just then, Golf flicked off the lights.

The room went black and she felt him grab her. His hands digging in to the plushness of her ass and his wet, dirty mouth kissing and biting against her neck and shoulders!

He panted: “Don’t fight it, Zora.”

One of his white fingers was plunging between the crack of her ass. Her panties, she felt, were being dragged off.

Her eyes bulged, swelling with tears, and she couldn’t speak or make a sound--she was so shocked to be getting what she had thought she wanted. Not sex. But just *man-woman attention* from a man that she was infatuated by and supposedly wasn’t good enough to have.

But she hadn’t expected it to feel this disrespectful, this dirty, and yet intellectually, *and by memory...*she had known that it would.

Her mind told her to scream. To make him stop.

Men like Golf had kicked holes in her father’s stomach and taken credit for the art that African people created. Men like Golf had called black mothers *apes* and taught little black boys to do the same. Men like Golf had raped little black girls and fully expected those little girls to behave as friends the very next day. Men like Golf knew about selfish greed. They knew all about people that were weaker than them.

You don’t deserve this! some voice inside Zorina seemed to be raging. But Noble was tearing her breasts loose now. Young and high they jiggled in his hands and got caught in his slobbering mouth! Zorina’s dress stank already, she realized, and it was smudged and soiled and torn, and so she merely braced the cold air as it came off. Her soft, hot flesh instantly being dug into by what seemed like the hands of many. He hurt her privates by wetting his fingers in her lips.

He didn't guide her to the bed--he bent her naked ass down to the floor.

Zorina wanted to stop him, but she didn't have the courage to stop him. She could feel her mother's slap against her face and she didn't know if she was good enough to demand to be treated with affection and tenderness.

"Oh, you sweet dirty little bitch," he moaned in ecstasy as he licked her neck, slobbered her mouth and bit at her nipples like a dog pup fighting to get milk.

There was no mention of her smelling like sunshine.

His thick white dick (penis, prick) went up in her.

The pain of it shooting through her body and ripping the tight skin of her pink opening. She was already bleeding.

His hand stifled the scream and her tears poured down the sides of her face, but she kept her weeping *restrained* so that no one would come and see what Golf really thought of her or find out how worthless a stain she really was.

She closed her eyes and tried to leave her body. She tried, desperately, to pretend that it was the kingish and very beautiful actor Djimon Hounsou inside her. Her favorite cinema idol. Then she could like it and want it.

But her mind wasn't strong enough to create all that.

It was Golf Theron banging her dirty little coffee stain!

Worthless kaffir trash bitch! That's what she called herself. Dirty, nasty little worthless piece of nothing.

nigger bitch.

Golf suddenly put his elbow in her mouth to brace the sound. Then he dramatically increased the swagger and the anxiousness of his beastfucking.

The pain shot through Zorina's body and she could hear the rhythm of the black boys as they chanted, rooting Golf on, cheering: "Funk-trunk pussy stain...bang, bang, bang." You have to get the flow of a rapper and picture a cute South African girl with a plump, tight ass and say it faster: "Funk-trunk pussy stain...bang, bang, bang!"

Funk-trunk pussy stain...bang, bang, bang!

Golf jumped up off her!

His dick was all bloody and he was coming.

He shoved his penis into Zorina's wet face and shot off his wad with a fierce stifled groan.

His chest heaved with heavy breathing and his wet, hot sticky jism ran in her eyes and all down the sides of her face.

"Wash yourself off, Zora...I got to git me rest, eh."

Golf was exhausted.

As Zorina lay on the floor, she could not seem to pull herself from the fire this time. Her classmates' screaming seemed to form a kind of chorus to a lullaby. The cinders were hot, but cold, too...this time. Eve smiled at her and handed her the knife. Eve kissed her on the cheek.

The knife?

Zorina didn't remember there being a knife in her hand, but suddenly, there was...and she was floating through the hotel's corridors. As if suspended just above the plush carpet.

In one hand she held the knife...and in the other...Golf Theron's white dick and his pink hairy sack; all bloody.

That seemed awfully odd.

Ugly, too. The sound of Maritza's high pitched screams.

Zorina ran out of the hotel.

The police hadn't put the bullet between her eyes yet.

So she ran...freer than she'd ever been. Down to the street til she reached the docks. She stood there...staring out at the shiny black sea.

Beautiful ocean...becoming more and more of itself.

She didn't hear the sirens of the police automobiles.

No. She heard the drunk blues woman singing from America: "*...that front porch...that's one dayyyn-jerus PLACE.*"

They called Zorina's name. So she turned around.

The gunshots sounded so far away; annoying.

So she turned back around.

She saw two people...walking on water! Walking right across the sea, swiftly coming towards her.

It was Jesus Christ with charcoal black Eve!

Coming to get her, she realized.

Jesus didn't look anything like the effeminate Christ that the whites always portrayed. He was tall and buff, dark like a Mexican or some other sexy latin breed of king...he had wet curly black hair and suave, sensuous bedroom eyes.

He reached out his hand to Zorina and said, "Don't be afraid of the way it feels..."

To her stunned surprise, she had already fallen into the water. But now Jesus Christ lifted her to her feet. She stood, quite astonished, atop the water's surface.

She and Eve embraced as tightly as long lost sisters!

"I hope you won't miss the fire," said Eve.

"I won't," said Zorina.

"We have a new life for you," said Nopopie, Zorina's father, as he stepped out of the fog...and into the moonlight. Zorina ran into his arms. She was so overjoyed!

"Oh, daddy," she cried. "Without a father, life is so hard!"

Then Jesus Christ, whose wet honey-bronzed chest stuck out like a shield of faith, asked her, "Do you have any last words before we leave this place?"

Zorina's eyes filled with tears, because for a moment, she felt human again. She thought of how some whites had often called black women *mules*. A mule is a small brown donkey that stinks and is considered ugly and used exclusively for servitude. A mule's stinking baby is called a mulatto.

"Yes...I do."

She turned and looked at the lights of the now crowded pier, legions of superior white faces around the ambulances, the fire brigades, South Africa's evil police.

From an *irrevocable* soul, Zora promised Jesus Christ: "The black woman...is the meteor...that is coming to this earth!"

From

Flesh and the Devil

Part One
"The Creation"

"There is no such thing...as the past, the present
or the future.
For they are all three...*simultaneous*."

--**King Kashta**
Ruler of ancient Sudan

Father

Before the White people created time and sailed on ships to bring it to us--*we lived forever.*

•

We were not that tribe of charcoal people that could fly...*no*...we were their neighbors, the deep dark brown people who could reside underwater for days at a time.

My name was Kofi, but I died when I was about nineteen from a rotten tooth.

I was a son of the swimmers that settled along the ocean in the roam of West African jungle and the black wombs of warm lakes. The charcoal people knew us to be fierce warriors and aggressive hunters. Imaginative, storytelling, superstitious men and women with muscular tombesque bodies, thick boar-sized buttocks, flat wide noses, wind-defying hair and fully everlasting lips. Our evil was more wicked than nary the most vicious hyena and our goodness was more godly than the creek of heaven in honey.

The charcoal people worshipped the sea, because they were afraid of it, and we, the sea dwellers, worshipped the sky, because we could not fly, and therefore, feared the wrath of both sun and moon.

Still, the flying tribe and the sea dwellers alike believed in the one true thing--*the story of creation.*

It is what kept us from war in the beginning, because our fathers talked about it and sang about it and told every generation about it each available moment.

I am not the only African who remembers so clearly.

Father would stand before the fire pit where mother roasted yams with whatever game he and his brothers had hunted down. He would be chewing on some fig or slice of kola nut and his chest would heave from the passion of his words as he taught us the story of creation (for all our lives, so we wouldn't forget), his brow always lifted to the universe as he said, "*The Sky was the man and the Sea...was the woman...and they hated each other!*"

Not just us children, but all the wise people listened whenever someone was telling the story of creation. The art of listening, whether it be to animal sounds, humans or wind and rain patterns, was considered one of the highest virtues of mankind in those times.

Father would explain, "*They hated each other, you understand, because there was no land, no earth back then, so they had no way of touching. It's the not being able to touch that keeps the griot man and the fire witch at one another's throats.*"

Mother would always splash a little water on her long, heavy breasts at that moment--pursing her lips and rolling her eyes at father.

"*Onward and forever, they were in a competition to see who was the most powerful one. The Sky would thunder and lightning, but never shed water, because the shedding of water would mean that he loved the Sea and this would give the Sea a victory. So instead, to slap her, the Sky would make fish-scooping, fire-breathing Pterodactyls appear or send giant evil fire rocks hurtling past the night moons and into the Sea. And the Sea would hiss and howl, because she had only one thing to impress the Sky with and that was her mysteriously dark depths that not even the sun and moons could see all the way to the bottom of, and she would tease him with the leaping of her dolphins and the blowing of her whales and the rainbow-reflecting beams of giant jellyfish, and still, with all her beauty...she was frustrated that she hadn't the power to reach up and touch the Sky."*

"So, of course, there had to be land...and one day, the Sky lost his advantage. He became anxious and alarmed, because he looked down and saw that the Sea had made a new creature...a dolphin with breasts!...leaping into the gold bars of the sun! It was a half woman, half fish--with a face dark and beautiful as hunter's ebony and with hair just like ours--a short, thick jungle that was powerful enough to hold the water and sun at the same time and not lay down, but be as an equal God against the elements."

"The Sky could not believe he was seeing such a beautiful creation! A thing whose eyes were of the sensitivity and intelligence of a seal and whose dolphin tail writhed with a sensuality. Zig-zagging through water slick and soulful as an eel. Teasing as it came and as it departed."

"He had to have her! But just as he devised it, the Sea told him--'None of my creations can survive in the Sky'--and with that, the half woman, half dolphin disappeared beneath the depths of the Sea like a wet dream."

••

*"The Sea named her daughter the word that now means LOVE in our language--**Ajowa**. And when the Sky heard her name announced, he was amazed and infuriated that he could not possess her...so this time he thought of a way he could touch the Sea--he would attempt to make a mountain rise out of her!...and to accomplish that, he would send no mere burning meteor to crash into the Sea...oh no...he would send one of the earth's two moons!"*

••

"The silver Moon and the white Moon, which together, were the Kindred Spirits. So this we rebuke three times. To make their love apart...to make their love apart...to make their love apart, because the Sky was mad."

And so the silver moon crashed into the sea of love while the white one remained high above. And this was the beginning--of touching.

"The Sea, you understand, was not powerful enough to brace the impact of the landing moon--for it tore through her depths like a million bolts of lightning, the round mighty power of it crashing to her floor and burrowing into the silk and satiny black mud from which she'd fashioned Ajowa. Bringing a great explosion, children! An explosion more fiery than sunburst! For it cracked into the womb of the world and pierced the earth's core and sent forth all the fires of all the dragons in the universes. And erupted...and erupted...until the Sea thought she must be dying."

"But she wasn't dying. She was giving birth! For out of her rose a great richness of black soil and solid rock, gases and fires that made a mountainous sloping valley of green and jungled majesty. For this would become Africa, the beauty released from the one moon, who was earthbound and bitter now--and its declaration of love to the other moon, who was heavenly and had turned against the Sky and vowed not to shine for a thousand years. A thousand years I will not shine, *it said to the Sky--and so the Sky and the Sea found their lights turned off, becoming completely black those first nights, seeping the one into the other as the stars dimmed to support the Moon...and there was nothing that could be seen or heard but darkness."*

"Ajowa...the woman who was half dolphin, rose out of the crater where the great explosion had taken place--and she came to the surface of the Sea--and she glowed as brightly as the golden bars of the sun...until there was light enough to make the night look like an orange sunset. This glow that radiated from inside Ajowa flowed like a fog across the hills and valleys of the newly formed land causing all manner of trees and fruit to spring up, and to punctuate her magic--she thought up butterflies--and set them loose in the jungles!"

"The Sky had never seen anything like it! He had to have her!"

He had to possess her! (I knew the story by heart)

"And so he made thunder and lightning from the Sky...and the Sea and her daughter thought it was merely a giant hail storm being released at first, but then...no...they thought it was a battalion of Pterodactyls. But then, no...it wasn't any creature they'd ever seen before. This one was a new one." Father would pause then, his eyes going from face to face before dramatically announcing, "*For the Sky had fashioned...a man.*"

And when father got to this part, we children always cheered and applauded! Such a wonderfully patriotic feeling would race through us!

Mother's pretty black face would be grinning and smirking, simultaneously, and our eyes would beam the size of saucers as we felt as if we were witnessing our own father men returning to the village once more after a hard day's hunt.

"*Yes, a man. Fully male with two legs, thick as pillars and muscular arms spanned out in flight, his hair as dense and wooly as Ajowa's and his skin blacker than hers--the color of charcoal. The Sea saw the penis between his legs and sent a fleet of sea horses to form a red splotch across her blue complexion as her most acrobatic dolphins flipped rings in acknowledgement of the man's beautiful penis and his muscled stomach and his measured flying...which was more graceful than a hawk's!"*

And then...all of a sudden, he did not belong to Sky.

"The man landed upon the earth and set his feet apart and poked out his black chest as though daring the sun to burn him, and he put his hands on his hips like this, and between his mighty, muscular legs hung his beautiful penis as though it were a sceptor of power and invincibility. He rose his head as though it were a crown and turned his powerful voice against the Sea...and said...'I am called God. I am called Master. Above all

the beasts, I am the greatest and the King. Comehither, Ajowa. Come and greet God'."

Into the Sea, he dared step his foot. Out into the tide he walked, as though from the Sea he had come.

"He stretched out his hand and commanded--I have been sent by my father, the Sky, to possess you. Now you must set aside your mother. You, the goddess of love, must leave the womb of the Sea. Come to me, Ajowa!"

But Ajowa's mother, the ocean, you understand...was not in agreement. For in West Africa, we had a saying: "*Count on the ocean--to find out women.*"

And thus the Sea rose up a tidal wave to kill God!

To rope his throat with seaweed so that she could drag him deep and drown him and snap his neck at the same time.

And as the Sea rose up a tidal wave, the Sky yelled down at her, "*You wet...bitter...bitch*! *I'll drop the red planet on your rolling blue ass*!"

But the Sea could not be intimidated. She summoned an army of all the sharks that had ever ripped birds out of flight and opened her floors so that volcanoes erupted into screaming, hissing hot whirlpools whose crushing throats would someday inhabit the earth as boa constrictors.

"And she realized then that because of the land...they could touch...and that the Sky wanted to enter her, as had always been the lamentation behind the Kindred light of the moons."

"To enter the Sea."

"To penetrate her depths as though the Sky owned them and were the God of them, and then leave her...the ocean...touched and left forever on the bottom. Forever on the bottom looking up at him!"

We boys would laugh at that part, but father would continue, "*You must understand that already...the Sea felt enslaved, because the Sky seemed, to her...endless, boundless and free."*

"So...the Sea...stood up!"

A tidal wave as high as any bird had ever flown! So high, in fact, that some of the Sky's fluffiest clouds were submerged underwater...not because woman was about to be entered...but because woman had not been entered before.(Father said that women, more than men, don't like "change.")

"Ajowa rose in the window of the Sea's wall of water--her body suspended in the S shape of a sea horse. Her curious seal's eyes beholding the passionate black gaze of God. Her curiosity pumping at the ecstasy of a creature who looked so close to her own image."

Father would pause and ask--"*Could the Sea have killed God?*"

We would only stare at him, wide eyed with our mouths ajar in wonder. We would nod.

"*Of course, she could have! But tell me...why didn't she?*"

My oldest brother would always bolt upright at that point and say, "Because the Sky gave her what she wanted."

"She wanted love," I would chirp right behind him.

"*And how...could the Sky give the Sea love?*"

"By raining!" we would all reply in unison, our hearts warmed by the one thing that all the generations and evolutions of Africans considered to be sacred and divine--rain.

"*Yes,*" father would say in a low, tender voice. And his black chest would be heaving as though he'd just been chased from the jungle by a cheetah.

He would say, "*The Sky stopped the Sea from killing God by giving her love. For the first time ever--he let it rain. Her own likeness falling upon her face as though she...the Sea...was being brought into the world all over again.*"

"And when it rained...the whole seed of our kind came into being. The Sea fell back in her ocean bed and let him in--and Ajowa swam freely to God, her tail splashing with joy as she anchored her hands against his ankles beneath the low tide, and with her mouth she kissed his penis--and then God lifted her up out of the water and carried her into the jungle...and as the rain fell upon the feast of their meeting, Ajowa shed her tail and she had legs! Smooth, beautiful satiny black legs that were soon parted by God. And he lay atop her and put the whole world inside her. And that was the beginning of the earth and humankind. And that was the first time that it ever rained. And that was the beginning...of our people's love story."

"BUT..."

Father raised a single finger here as if to say--the story isn't over. Then, somberly, "*What is love...without a curse*?"

How can there be "*love*"...without a curse?

••

The grown ups always nodded, immediately, because if there's one damnable thing African people obsessed about, it was love. Father would nod his head, too, and proceed to finish the story as though none of us had ever heard it before. "*The poor Moon of course...was very angry and vengeful. Hanging solitary in the dark of night--so that the Sky and the Sea could touch via land and make love through man and woman."*

"And when the night became a blanket covering God and Ajowa's lovemaking--the Moon broke its vow to not be seen for a thousand years--and it showed itself to be so full and bright that it nearly blinded them. And they stood up before it, their naked black beauty sealed in the Moon's ivory glow, and the Moon said...'I curse you!'"

"I curse you Man and Woman and shall wring out of you children."

And as the Moon said this, Ajowa began to bleed betwixt her legs!

"I curse thee that your children will know the heartbreak and sorrow that your parents, Sky and Sea have burdened on me."

"That you stole my love...and hindered my light."

"I send my curse on the wings of the owl for all the evenings that are yet to grace this bitter earth. And you shall hear my sobbing in this world forever, and I will not go away for a thousand years...but I will watch you be born and take death...each and every Night...till tomb."

"For I am no longer part of the two who were kindred, but am now just half of misery."

"O misery!, cried the Moon. *"Where is my company?"*

"Half a moon. Half a moon."

"My curse be upon thee!"

Man and Woman. Sky and Sea.

1,000 Years Later

Mother

My name was Soraya, and although I died giving birth to my seventeenth child when I was twenty-seven...I remember being in the world back when we humans were astonished and baffled by the sight of the very first "*white baby.*"

None of us remembered flying or living underwater anymore.

My days were the days when the offspring of the flying man (God) and the goddess of love (Ajowa) would join as one in a common ritual--the lifting into the Sky of all newborn children so that they received the blessing of the full moon.

••

The charcoal clan (the Gods) and the more-chocolate-than-blood clan (the Ajowans) had long forgotten the original story of creation. They had separate beliefs now and this sometimes brought the two tribes to war. The Gods believed that the first human was a warrior called Bayajidda who fell to earth from the Moon so as to search for his lost love--Daura (*the one who is lonely, the one who is calling us*). And because the

Moon was so pleased to see longing and loneliness united as one, it had anointed the lovemaking of Bayajidda and Daura and let rain fall upon them, spilling the earth with children.

The Ajowans, however, were insulted by that story. They insisted that everything came from the Sea.

They taught their children that a great mean shark and a young sweet dolphin had broken the laws of nature by not swimming away from each other, but by falling in love. An *"inter-species"* love so unnatural and impossible, testified the Ajowan griot men, that the Moon above took pity on the animals and turned them into a new creature--*humans*--and brought them out of the Sea to live on land.

And the first man had taken the name that meant Wise One, provider and father--Kofi. And the first woman took the name that meant fertility, obedience and motherhood--Iyanla. And when they made love, it erupted a great approval of pouring rain from the sky and clouds...and from then on, the Ajowan people decreed by law that all its Kings be named Kofi and that all the Queens of Kofi be called Rain Iyanla.

And that became the tradition of the Ajowans.

••

So in my lifetime, you understand, there was no memory of the Moon's curse upon mankind or of the old days when the Gods and the Ajowans had slaughtered children as human sacrifices, presenting their bloodied necks as dowry for the moon's forgiveness. Those days had ended--because the first white child in history had been born!

A blue eyed, orange haired boy that their ancestors had named Foghu (the living dead). They called him "*the living dead*" because his flesh was obviously too pale to have blood in it and because his eyes seemed flat and soulless like a shark's.

His birth, however, had been absolute proof to the conjure men of both tribes that the curse was lifted. The Moon had accepted their sacrifices and forgiven Africa by sending a white baby--obviously, a *moon* baby.

"Now we must give him to the Sea," decreed the highest holy man of the Ajowans. "For this is no mere human child, but a deity. We must worship him!"

"*Worship him!*" screamed the voices of both nations as their torches of fire were lifted against the blackness of night and their cheering ululations drowned out the cries of the white baby as his throat was slit.

To all the people of all the clans in both nations, this seemed a righteous end, because there was not a single moment that a single one of them imagined that such a special oddity--a white baby from the moon--could remain living as a mortal amongst humans. Obviously, he was to be worshipped.

So they deified, as well...his charcoal mother, a cassava picker from the lower classes, and they proclaimed him a new name--Piru Nu (King of the Sharks) and they contracted the greatest artists and craftsmen from both tribes to fashion a sacred chair, ten feet tall and four feet wide.The inner compartments of the chair having room for the bodies of both mother and child as the infant one was placed at her living black breast and anointed with the beads and amulets of all the kings, queens and spirit men of both nations and then cast into the Sea--a floating ark.

In those days we were grateful to Piru Nu and erected a great totem in the temples of both cultures, honoring him once a year by covering our faces, arms and chests with white ash and dancing a new dance--the dance of the sharks. In honor of his mother, because she had resembled a monkey in the face, we wouldn't eat monkey meat for an entire month!

And that was back then.

••

I remember witnessing another miracle when I was just a little girl on my honeymoon night.

As my husband slept on top of me, the coolness of earth beneath us, I had awakened, finding it difficult to breathe, and had slipped from under him and went out of the hut, hoping to find a fresh gust of air.

But it turned out that the sprawl of African evening was even more humid, and it seemed that somehow...the *Moon* was burning down against the jungle. Hotter than any sun I'd ever walked under. Languid and thick as a wild dog's lust just before it mounts and rapes a sheep.

I became entranced by its power and anger, and there seemed to be a creamy yoke of smoke wafting around the pearl of its white glow.

I heard a *moan* that only a black woman can make. Tear-sugared and caterpillar velvet like a note she had meant to sing but choked on.

I was freshly de-virginized that night, the ache and the blood between my tiny swollen pussy like a rash...but still, I was a little girl and I didn't really know about sex or passion or *the art* that makes delirium cook a couple's lovemaking like honey seared by brimstone.

Crackling sticks under foot, I tiptoed barefoot along the cool earth, toward the pretty moaning, and went down a path that lead to a shiny, shiny...*shiny* black lake.

My mouth parted when I saw them.

The shadow space of a man and a woman so black you could see the whole world being made.

His muscles wrapped around her shoulders like a python embracing the beating heart of a doomed swan, and yet her throat (*such a long throat*!) let go of the moans...the fervor and beauty of each one resembling some part of musicality, but too indecent to abide singing.

Everything about it--was beautiful and wet.

The light rain, hot enough to make steam as it pelted the black lake...and the dripping white sperm of the moon. Yes, *dripping* like your age's candlewax, falling hot and white across their black embrace, their black kiss, their black dance, their black need. Cursing and hissing as it fell from out of the Moon--like spit. Upon grace.

Moonlight. Watching the fuck.

And my own young body trembling, the bell of woman's damnation throbbing in my stomach like a growing need to urinate...as I saw her fall slow like insects do when they die in flight, her body taking to earth with the yield of a female panther, her dark shadow creating the canvas...for dreams.

And I could tell by the way that he navigated her bones and curves, and by the way that she moaned so soulfully, that they really loved each other. And that, somehow, their love was not a living love...but a love from where I am now, in the land after life...the other side. An eternal love.

It had something to do with me and all mankind, the slapping *fart sounds* that I heard as he fucked and kissed her at the same time, their necks twisting like vines up a tree; his eyes closed, hers open to stare at him; the shards of creamy moon jism smelling like sea anemones and burning jungle gardenia as it hit their cooking dance and steamed with the shiny shine of the lake.

It rained African rain...and the drops were sweet as sugar!

And once I could smell the fresh wildness of her pussy, and mistook it for oysters, I wanted it, too--him inside me. To take me and twist me and love me that way. I wanted it, too. But the closer I moved towards them, the more I saw the shine of the lake. The light playing tricks on me and my heart beating like a drum, louder and louder with each step I took.

When I got there, it was just children...*kids*! Two black, bony little naked Africans wrestling and laughing. Two boys for all I could tell, but no...I don't know.

I hated myself for years for not staying where I was, because I never saw them again. Or felt the beautiful energy that shined out of them like points of light flickering in a lavender diamond.

And I never got a taste of what she got, but always fantasized that perhaps in some other lifetime I might find him...touch him...next lifetime.

••

Children of Africa will remember that our parents explained romantic love between a man and a woman in an animalistic way. They called it--"the insanity."

"It comes over you," they would say, "like heat stroke or rabies or a lion leaping out of a bush. You have use of your mind, but the feeling is so powerful, you dismiss your mind. You are high from the insanity. It's too good to let it go. Your insecurity needs it, your mind needs it, your body craves it. Your soul, which comes from the other side and not from this world, remembers it. The insanity. It is not a *growing* love."

But being a female, I didn't get to choose the man that I felt "*the insanity*" for. I had to marry the one who paid my parents dowry...and in time, I *grew* to love him and need him and respect him and cherish him...and there was nothing insane about it, but our parents called this kind of love--*growing love*--and this was the kind they meant when they said, "Love wisely...not...insanely."

But wise or not, I can never forget the way that the shadow man's charcoal hands handled the sloping curves of the panther woman's charcoal body. She may as well have been one of those violins the Europeans caress with their chins or a precious stone from under the sea mud. There was something more naturally human than humanly civil about it. And yet, the two of them together, had rocked my soul and melted the Moon.

••

Only in death have I appreciated my name. Soraya--*the observant one.*

Tonight, I am watching the ritual again.

The *"Night of the Living"* festival.

The Gods and the Ajowans coming in legion, by foot, by oxen, by royal carry platter and by the thousands, the Gods dressed in flowing chains of cowrie shell, gold nugget neck collars and ebony-carved masks while the Ajowans came buff and naked with ornate headdress and red clay-painted faces...the ritual congregating along the coastline of the Ajowan's great city, Mars. There they stood, the torch bearing architects of the modern world--a thousand years removed from the lovemaking of God and Ajowa. No longer remembering that there ever existed a curse or a white moon baby to remove it, and certainly no such legend as a flying underwater time when there was...*no such thing*...as time.

I was always there for the ceremony in Mars.

Three Ngba girls (God virgins) and three Mars girls (Ajowan virgins), united only for that night by a white dot on their foreheads, walked as bare skinned slaves into the ocean tide clutching poisonous berries in their hands and raising their voices in harmony as their young eyes fastened on the Moon, their dutiful suicides by sea lying the foundation as the God nation and the Ajowan nation stood for all humanity and unbound the ritual of call and response:

"*We come from the Moon*!" sang the Gods. And their legions of tall, thin sinewy charcoal men raised the newly born sons of their nation above their heads and presented them to the full moon.

"*We come from the Sea*!" replied the Ajowans. And the new fathers amongst their pure chocolate adonis men raised the newly born sons above their heads and presented them to the moon.

Each father let a little blood from his son.

Erupting from silence, the women of both nations ululated wildly, their noise growing until it was epic enough to scare all animal life out of the jungle's light and into deeper blackness, the ivory moonglow glistening against the long, bouncing titties of the ebony brown Ajowans and reflecting as silver against the bare elegant shoulders and blue black faces of the charcoal God women.

The King of the God people and the Kofi of the Ajowans then came together, each one bearing a wooden female doll in whose belly compartment their great spirit men had placed the richest, darkest soil from the most sacred earth representing each of their finest growing fields.

The King of the God people took a nugget of his dirt and placed it in the waiting mouth of the Kofi leader, saying, "I give you the mother."

Then as the Kofi leader was eating the dirt in his mouth, he took a cluster of Ajowan soil and placed it on the tongue of the God King and reciprocated by saying, "I give you the mother."

All Africa cheered as the Kings ate dirt.

And on the body of Ajowa, African soil, stood the whole world of humanity. Where it had always stood.

That much they did remember.

••

By the time my sixteenth child was born, my breasts were hanging long and flat as curtains of raw liver. Milk dripped against my waist from the nipples...and huge green flies gathered on my hip bone to drink it.

I would swat them from the precious faces of my babies, and from my face as well. My curious gaze always longing for that secret door that opens and shuts at any given moment in black children's eyes. I call it the soul door, because it's not just silver light atop black inky eyes...*no*...black children are celestial-eyed.

Black children are celestial-eyed.

I was Soraya--*"the one who is observant"*--and I gave birth to seventeen healthy, mud-fine, jungle-nappy sons and daughters. And let me tell you...

Black children are celestial-eyed.

Everything that ever was and everything that ever will be...is in their eyes. They look just like God. Living and dreaming at the same time.

And that...was why I wanted him to exist, you understand.

Me, Soraya.

I wanted him. Not my village husband...but *him.*

••

Black women always want *him.*

That's all we want. That's why our pussy is so sweet.

Hoping it's him coming out of our good wild stinky stuff.

Even at the start of the world, when African women laid around naked in dens hugged up with other women, it was that part of *him* that's in a woman's "plans" that we wanted. Like the white lizard seeking honeysuckle, we will do anything...dream trees into being, dream up new colors until the sky shows them off, make drinks out of fallen rain and slash our pussies with jagged rocks, stitching them tight and tiny. Put plates in our mouths and stretch our lips and ears past our knees--like slaves used to do back east.

Walk into the sea swallowing poisoned berries.

Weep and weep...because only we know that no woman can love a man like a black woman can. Yet...it's the finding him.

And even if they never find him, African girls are *walking* women. That's why the African maiden is the least obese on the planet, even surpassing the strong but boy-shaped Asian in "harmony of shape." She walks everywhere.

Because the village mothers told her, "Do not...look for *him*!"

But there are so few of *him*...that he almost never exists anyway.

So while the other village mothers were saying, "You'll never find him," I decided that it made more sense to just...give birth...to him.

As an African woman, let me tell you...this is the greatest earthly power that any woman has. The power...*to give birth to the people that she needs*. And you will notice that whenever a woman forgot that power, she was alone.

I wanted him.

I wanted him for my daughters and for their daughters and for the whole world of sweet, sad women. I dreamt a dream for them.

While my husband was on top of me, and while my sixteen children slept in ground dug-out floors, their bodies safely netted from insects, I dreamt *"him"* into being. His body forming in my uterus like a curl of smoke--no, it was more like sea mist and wind song. The bones in his back not coming until my husband collapsed atop my black ocean of a body, sweating profusely, his moan enchambering me with a helplessness...and the cut and tied-together muscles of my pussy clutching and clenching his staff...so as to milk out every precious drop of the new king.

I wanted him...so that other women could be touched by dreams, and so that the love in us could fill the earth with our longing.

So that there could be insanity.

But my only mistake was that in *longing* for love...I had become insane. And that night, when I left my husband sleeping in the hut and went out into the moonlight...I was startled by a sudden, sharp slap across my face.

It felt like my mother's old black hand. Stinging the shit out of my cheek as the fingers and the palm of it, invisible as air, just flung out of nowhere and popped me across the face, hard and belligerent!

"*Insufferable fucking humans*!"

In shock I held my cheek, the pain bringing tears to my eyes as my heart began to beat like a drum.

I looked up at the Moon, its galaxy-bright whiteness so overwhelming that I thought it would blind me, and with each breath...I knew that I was insane and that I had been slapped and that I was pregnant with it, my *dream*, and that the Moon wanted to reach down and rip it out of me.

But I held my belly and I loved my dream; I loved it.

"*Love and dreams belong to me,*" said the Moon.

I shook my head, delirious with ecstacy. I said, "No...I am woman. I am the mother of God. I am more powerful than the Moon. My dreams belong to me!"

The Moon laughed and said, "Then dream about this."

And when I fell backwards...I fell awake.

••

It became a pregnancy licked by tape worms.

The right hand of the fetus grew huge and knuckle-fisted inside me, clutched and vicious as the giant claw of a stone crab. Beating me. Ripping my flesh inside. Socking and punching with each new morning.

In the sun's hot work day, pounding grain with my youngest child strapped to my back, I bent over cramped in pain, my eyes filling with tears as my heart--the heart of a mother--ripped like silk webs.

He opened his ass and shit all inside me.

With feet of brass, he kicked and stomped against my walls as though trying to make a window.

I couldn't sleep at night, because his nappy headed skull would shake like a Pagomba rattle, his scream lit in my ears and mind like the bright fury of a meteor shower. His kicking and punching...*killing me*.

It rained the night he was born. Pure, sweet African rain.

"She's becoming very sick," I heard my husband wince to the circle gathered around my garden bed.

"She's been bleeding for two weeks!" my sister complained.

"She's going to die," said Seed Smoker, the old family griot. "The baby's inside her, fucking her."

"No...not my Soraya. She's strong as a lioness!"

"There's too much love in her, Akiffo. Too much love kills a woman. They go insane."

Seed Smoker lifted his sharpest stone. "I'm going to have to take the baby, Akiffo. One of them is not going to make it."

He made a few incisions, and then as he fought to get control of the swinging and kicking baby boy, the child lunged out with a mouth full of sharp teeth and bit deep into my vagina. Biting clamp-jawed like a pit bull. But by then I was already dead, and in death, powerful enough to choke the muscles of his infant throat to a crushing close, the walls of my vagina twisting the soft bones of his skull like clay rolls as my ambilical cord snapped his wind pipe and popped out his left eye.

"...eeek!" he went, and that's what mothers are for, too.

"Lost them both," said Seed Smoker.

••

Into the bright blue yonder I went...both cloud of the Gods and roaring riptide of the Ajowans attending my train like sea mist and wind song. My black, black arms cradling the beautiful healthy Prince...my kiss against his dark face in tender victory, because the Moon had not won. *I* had won.

I had brought my dream into being.

My precious, precious insanity...with his gently kicking feet, his halo of nappy African hair and his celestial, ever-timeless dark eyes. His sweet, sweet smile laughing up at my soul like the shimmering twinkle on nightwater.

To the edge of heaven I went...to its ocean.

I knelt down and placed his divine body into the cradle of the sea, and of course, he took to water like a bolt of lightning.

Earth shatteringly! Defiantly!

Eternally.

My love.

Oh!...

my...love!

The Kingdom of AjowaLand

Several Thousand Years Later

Chapter 1

A man, at sixteen, must marry--but the Sea wanted Prince Shango Ogun all to herself.

Warriors from his father's vast army stood about the shoreline now, informing him that they had been sent by his parents to escort him to the royal stool at once, but Shango dove beneath the water's clear window pane, deliberately ignoring them, his body spiraling downward like a dolphin's. He despised his nation's edict that he must now choose a bride, because if there was to be any marriage, then Shango would rather it be between himself and the Sea. Shango wasn't just a Prince and a loner, he was a dreamer, and in order to dream, he needed to be underwater by himself.

These were still the days, you understand, when the Sea could gently masturbate the genitals of those who swam inside her, her silky tickling waters en-mouthing the swimmer's sensitivity...or...a favorite plant, touched by the hand of its dearest one, could ejaculate warm jism, filling the jungle garden with birth odor and tilly bees, their droning stingers poking butterflies into falling deaths of ecstasy...or a warrior bathing in the stream at midnight could find the tight tender pucker of his asshole, as he bent to wash the bottom of his foot, delicately beam-fingered by a ray of hot moonlight.

The natural cleanliness of the sensual world was still so pure and wild back then, so overwhelmingly dominated by spirit lust and sheep laughter that human beings preferred to do most of their living outdoors, their sun burnt black bodies brushed up against by playful virgin breezes or wedges of sun, juicy-thick as daydreams or *rain*...blue and artful as the children it drenched. Shango Ogun loved it all and wanted nothing more from the earth.

"Royal Prince...royal prince!" the soldiers called as they followed Shango's swimming dark shadow along the shoreline. "You will get us in trouble if you do not come along peaceably. It has been two weeks since you ignored your father's summons!"

Shango could stay underwater for incredible lengths of time or could suddenly lightning bolt himself out to deeper sea, and thus figuring that one of them had better do something fast, one of the smarter soldiers hollered out, "This situation is taking its toll on your beloved grandmother!"

The other men looked at the lying soldier with pause as he continued shouting, "It's breaking your grandmother's heart! She's been crying all the day and all the night, worried that..."

Immediately...Shango Ogun sprang up from the sea, the sea rolling down his body like sheaths of mirrors as the smartly lying soldier thought to himself--"*what a perfect name that Hoodi, the ruling Kofi of Ajowa and his beautiful* queen, *Rain Iyanla, have given their son.*" For as much as the soldier was jealous of Shango's privileged status, he could not deny that the impassioned idealism of the Prince did remind him of thunder (Shango) and that the massive span of the sixteen year old's chest, the heavy black fruit of his loins and the pillar-like muscularity of his legs could have very well been inspired by iron (Ogun). He was bigger and stronger than one third the warriors in Kofi Hoodi's army, noticed the soldier. Yes, thunder and iron (Shango Ogun) was the perfect name for him.

"It is normal," said the smart soldier to the approaching Prince,"...for a young man to be nervous about the business of choosing a proper wife." As the smart soldier said this, his eyes darted in and out of Shango's stare as if he were more fit to be royalty than the one born into it. His mouth saying, "A concubine can be any stray desire, but *a wife* must bare the fruit of his family's blood and bring back to life all its greatest men. A wife gives us life forever."

Shango said nothing as he boarded the terracotta carry platter upon which he would sit as the elephant carried him back toBanjula City.

"And tell us," asked the smart soldier with a smile to the handsome prince. "Which one of the virgins is qualified to stand behind you, young master?"

"Silence!" the sixteen year old commanded the older man. "I don't wish to share my thoughts today. I'd rather be underwater."

"Yes, *0* master."

The elephant was raised and made to move with a fey slap across the hinds. And onward bound they went, up from the beach and into the jungle and beyond the clay cliffs and grass flats, their trek taking them past the ruins of their once great city, Mars. Only the ancient totems stood there now and a few of the iron pits where their ancestors had once made rubber from the gum arabic plants they purchased from the ear-stretched, plate-mouthed Africans of the interior.

"Fan my chest."

"Yes, *0* master."

••

Yes, 0 master.

The words lingered in Shango Ogun's mind, because there handn't been a single day in his life when he hadn't heard one of his potential brides address him that way. These were the "nobility virgins"--the daughters of rich men who had been born on the same day as Shango Ogun, but four years after him. They had been sold by their fathers to the Kofi Hoodi, as was the practice when the son of a King was born, and raised up with Shango thereafter to be his loyal servants and to be groomed and tutored in the ways of royal marriage by Shango's grandmother, Mother Iyanla. Now he would have to carry out the ritual of *OorUtu*...a marriage rite that required him to penetrate the virginity of each girl in a single night and then choose one of them to be his royal wife while the others were runner ups to the status of concubine to the Prince and servant to the wife.

Shango found it to be a thankless and painful decision to make, because after growing up with all five girls as his servants and playmates, he had truly come to love and appreciate each one for her own special uniqueness.

Tandi, the prettiest one, and the one his father liked best, was round and very thick as the Ajowans preferred their women. She had rich ebony smooth skin like Shango's mother, large oval shaped almond brown eyes hooded by long peacock lashes and about her the most--Shango loved her smile. It was brighter than the sun, but still, she was not his favorite one.

His mother's pick, Keisha, was extremely black-skinned (which meant, as many African tribes believed, that her womb would be more likely to produce an abundance of athletic warrior boys as opposed to sentiment sons or girlchilds), and she, too, was soft, cushy and thick, but her interest was more in sitting up under his mother than going with him underwater to catch crabs.

Beeni was the intellectual one. She liked to go down to the abandoned lion's dens and read their foot prints to see who they had been in a past life. She also had gigantic breasts and had fascinated Shango all his life with her stories about the baboon elves that lived up under them. Anat, the skinny one, was the finest cook and the most artistic, but then again, she talked incessantly and hated swimming.

That left only his grandmother's favorite--Soraya.

Soraya was the quiet, observant one. She had light honey colored skin, which was extraordinarily rare and was considered by many tribes to be the sure sign of a spirit living halfway in the human world and halfway in the next world, or as the Ajowans would say--"*the color doesn't show all the way because the person's spirit lives in two worlds, simutaneously, without committing to either*"--and because these rare light skinned people tended to darken in old age (a sign that they had finally chosen the tribe), it was believed that they were magnets for good spiritual luck and prosperity, so this was why Mother Iyanla told her grandson, "Soraya will bring peace to your house. She will bear healthy sons and be a warm cushion beneath your feet. It's been a hundred years since our family had a good luck bride."

Shango Ogun nodded to himself now--then Soraya it is, grandmother. And yet, he was very sad.

"What is this sadness, great Prince?"

"I'm too lonely to be married," muttered Shango, thoughtfully.

And upon his arrival at the mud flats which led to the walls of Banjula City, his saddened eyes fell upon the very poor lower classes and his brow raised, because it was quite obvious that the entire minion was waiting to glimpse him as he returned to his father's stool.

"What's going on here?" Shango asked the smart soldier as the others guided his elephant down the road. Shango had never seen anything like it. The poor and disadvantaged were everywhere, their usually overworked bodies separated from their tasks, bare breasted women with babies strapped to their backs and baskets atop their heads, their shiny black eyes staring up at him as murmuring voices announced that the Prince was passing through, but not a single smile or nod. Just curiosity and fear. "Why is everyone out to greet me? Why are they looking at me that way?"

"There's been a miracle since you've been gone," replied the smart soldier, guardedly. "A great...unbelievable...shocking...miracle, *0* master."

"What is this you say?"

"I cannot explain it to you, Prince Shango. It is up to your father and the Spirit Rulers to explain it."

Shango's blood raced and he felt fearful and nervous, because in all his life, he had never seen the people so united by murmur and stare. He picked up his drum from the drum holder and began to beat a message to his father...

the Prince is arriving at Banjula City. I want to know of the great miracle before then! I am not a baby, tell me what has happened?

But after he beat it out and the echo of it was played again and again by a network of drumming black hands, the message being passed up the road, village to village, until it surely reached his father's house...there was no reply from either the Kofi or his drummers.

Someone is dead, thought Shango. Why else would there be no reply? They were afraid, obviously, to tell him something. His heart began to beat wildly. *Grandmother*? Sheer terror gripped Shango's handsome face. He leaped from the carrying platter!

The soldiers were caught off guard and looked at him like he was crazy as he bolted towards the southern walls of Banjula City fast and furious, his rugged voice calling out, "Mother Iyanla!, Mother Iyanla!"

It was just a miracle. Plain and simple.

••

Within half an hour, Shango reached the walls of the stone courtyard of the royal compound of the reigning Kofi, his father, Hoodi. *He couldn't believe what he saw*! More than three thousand people were lining the road leading to the Kofi's compound and all around it they were stretching their necks as if to get a better view as they whispered awe-filled remarks. Shango dashed along the route, his thunderous voice announcing his royal status as he parted the civilians and soldiers blocking the entrance way. Then upon entry, he saw the Spirit Rulers of the Ajowan nation gathered already out in front of the clan porch, their heads bowed in prayer.

Royal Guardsmen beat a quick drum message to alert the Kofi and Rain Iyanla that their son had arrived, and immediately, the Spirit Rulers came out of prayer and the women of the clan began to descend from the cluster of cone dwellings, all dressed in their finest gold, pearl and cowrie jewelry, their bare breasts glistening beneath painted faces and elaborate geles.

Shango stopped in his tracks, because he saw his grandmother, Rain Iyanla--alive and well!--exiting the huts with a huge joyous smile on her face and clasping her hands together at the place where her long, flat breasts drooped beyond her waistline. She was followed by all five of his potential brides, and after them came his father's concubines.

Shango's mother, the Queen of Ajowa, Rain Iyanla, then sashayed out, her plump round chocolate body animated by regal confidence. She, too, was smiling, her hands raised in the air as she clacked together finger bells and proclaimed, "Our son has returned to witness it. For our people have been chosen to host a miracle!"

Shango gave a blank stare of confusion, but then coming behind his mother, a young girl--a girl that he'd never seen before in his life--appeared in the doorway of the largest cone hut and then sauntered out, nervously. She was carrying what appeared to be the shape and movement of an infant wrapped in a royal kinte cloth, but what truly alarmed Shango was that a girl of her status would be in the company of his mother, because she was quite obviously a dirt eating girl from the lower classes (and no one had memory of the old days when Kings ate dirt).

Shango stared at her, quizzically. Her head was not shaven or decorated with spirit paint or expensive ornaments as was the style for proper women of upper class Ajowan society. Instead, she wore her hair thick and full like a cloud of black cotton, and her skin was jet black and swarthy from an obviously hard life picking cassava in the sun jungles. Her features were thin and spare. She had no voluptuous lips, no feminine bald head, no sexy flat wide nose as pure Ajowans did.

"*This is Namibia,*" Rain Iyanla whispered to her son, urgently--she whispered, of course, because her husband was about to be presented to preside over the courtyard and the legions of onlookers who crowded the compound walls. Rain Iyanla leaned into her son's ear and reported quickly, "*Namibia is from a poor family in the mud villages...Namibia, this is my son, Prince Shango Ogun of Ajowaland.*"

And when Namibia raised her eyes to meet his for what seemed a micro-moment, Shango found himself strangely humbled by the plain attractiveness of the lower class girl. In her dark eyes he saw a meekness that eluded even the most obedient virgins from rich families. She was very natural.

As was custom for a first meeting between royalty and a commoner, Namibia dropped down to her knees, securing her infant as best she could, and bowed her head to kiss the top of the Prince's feet, the right foot first, because it represented the Kofi's good health, and the left foot second (and longer), because it represented her blessings and well wishings for the ongoing seed of the family's penis.

Just as Rain Iyanla and Mother Iyanla helped Namibia back to standing on her own feet, the drum roll began for the presentation of the Kofi.

She and Shango exchanged a locked glance, but then Namibia lowered her eyes as though she were inferior.

By mere chance, Shango looked over at his row of potential virgin brides and caught sight of Soraya, the light honey colored girl that he intended to choose as his bride since his grandmother liked her so much--he thought--*"that's odd, why is she staring at me with tears in her eyes as though she will never see me again?"*

Soraya said with her eyes, "I love you...goodbye."

And a chill went through his body.

••

Rain Iyanla rose the titchi totem feathers over her head and announced, "Let us be joined as the nation of Ajowa!" The soldiers and gathered civilians rose their right firsts into the air and responded, resoundingly, "*Ajowa*!" Then Rain Iyanla banged the totem three times against the clan porch. The Spirit Rulers bowed their heads and the women ululated.

Shango's father, the Kofi (King) of Ajowa, Hoodi, emerged from the cone hut like a great giant polar bear dipped and rolled in black oil. His hair was braided up in a hundred thumb-sized plats and his beard was white with chalk, his flesh taut and mealy as he dug his staff into the floor and sat upon his throne. He instructed Namibia to go and stand next to the Prince, which annoyed Shango instantly, because it was becoming clearer and clearer that they were somehow connecting this strange girl with the baby to him.

Shango's eyes shot against his father's face, demanding an explanation, but Kofi Hoodi casually took a drink of the palm wine offered by one of his concubines and ignored Shango's stare as he flipped ground nuts in his mouth and leaned on his right side once or twice to let out a loud, pungent fart. No one dared say a word. On the right of him sat Rain Iyanla and Mother Iyanla, their hands in their laps as Shango's virgins stood behind the Queen and grandmother, tall and straight. To the left of Kofi Hoodi were his concubines and the children, most of them grown, that he had fathered in all sundry.

Kofi Hoodi looked down at his son and the poverty stricken cassava girl. He said to the girl, "Show my son the miracle."

Namibia turned towards Shango and pulled back the kinte cloth that protected her baby from the hot rays of the sun. Shango looked down at the bundle, barely interested, but once he saw the baby's face--he winced and twisted up his own face, considering the child to be deformed. It had white flesh, white as ivory, and its eyes were blue like the secret part of the ocean and its hair was straight like a wild pig's.

"What is *that*!?" spat Shango with disgust.

"It's a baby," laughed Kofi Hoodi. "A white baby--sent to us from the next world!"

Shango looked to the line of plum black Spirit Rulers and they nodded in agreement with the Kofi. One of them said, "It is a miracle greater than any we've ever known, dear Prince. The child was pulled from Namibia's womb just three days ago. We have asked the Creators for knowledge and guidance and they have told us through dreams that the child's name is Bono."

"But...how can a human be white? There's no such thing."

"That's why it's a miracle!" thundered Kofi Hoodi. "This child is the living dead! Not among the God tribe but among *us*--the Ajowans! This child anoints us."

"Where is the child's father?" Shango asked the girl, but she only stared at him as though she feared for her life. Kofi Hoodi laughed and told the girl, "Tell him...tell my son who the father is."

Trembling and tearful, Namibia said, "*I was raped...by the moon.*"

Then she handed the baby to one of Hoodi's concubines and showed to Shango the marks on her body that had been made by the moon. On both her breasts there were bright splotches where her copper black skin had turned completely white and seemed to be glowing from within. Shango was shocked as he saw the same glowing splotches on her belly, her right wrist and the "glow" of others hidden between her legs. She came to tears and said, "*It happened two weeks ago*."

"But no one has ever been born in just two weeks!"

"*Isn't it a miracle*!?" Rain Iyanla enthused. "The moon has raped this child and anointed our people with a symbol of greatness!"

At that precise moment, the baby began to heave and cry, his little white hand balled up into a fist and swinging around as though demanding to be fed immediately. Shango looked closely at the back of the child's hand and noticed that there was hair growing from it like a monkey.

"He grows at an alarming rate," muttered Namibia, her eyes lowered in shame as she tried to place her nipple in the baby's screaming mouth, only to have him push the nipple away and holler louder. She knew what he wanted, but was too embarrassed for people to see.

"Give him the monkey bones!" cheered Kofi Hoodi with a boisterous laugh. "He's a growing hunter, his hunger is like that of a lion cub's."

Shango was about to object, to suggest that a newborn baby had not the teeth nor the strength to chew cooked meat let alone something so dangerous, splintery and hard as a monkey bone, but before he could say it, his father's concubine handed a bunch of thick monkey bones to Namibia--the baby literally grabbing the bones from the concubine before Namibia could pass them to his impatient clutch.

His pink mouth yawned to reveal large sharp white canine-like teeth and a red sticky cat-like tongue. *Crunch, crunch.* His powerful jaws began devouring the bones as though they were as soft as swamp weeds. His large egg-shaped head rising out from the kinte clothe like a full moon and his giant blue eyes bulging, the glassy flatness of them terrifying Shango as the child looked him square in the face and chomped down the bones, simutaneously.

Horror-struck, Shango looked to his grandmother for input, but she seemed to be as smitten with the baby as everyone else was.

"This is the secret weapon we've always prayed for," said Kofi Hoodi with a menacing raised fist. "Never before have we been able to defeat the God tribe in war. Peace and brotherhood have been our only options." Mother Iyanla looked away from the Kofi at that moment, her soul sickened by her son's lifelong desire for conquest. She thought of all the dead people's skulls that hung around the walls of the royal huts as though they were nothing more than seashells. Her son saying, "But now...now we have a warrior who will possess the strength of ten men and surely the magic of the moon and stars! This royal child will lead us to victory and domination!"

"Royal child?" Shango asked his father.

"But, of course, Shango. Bono is to be your son."

Shango's mouth fell open. His eyes opened wide with dismay. My son? He looked pleadingly to his grandmother, his stare insisting that she intervene on his behalf, but all she said was, "It has been brought to your father by the Spirit Rulers...word from the creators, Shango...that our people must keep this child and raise him as an Ajowan. He is a gift to us."

Shango began to shake his head. "No."

"You are blessed!" thundered Kofi Hoodi. "You are to be the future Kofi of Ajowa. You must take Namibia as your bride and future Rain Iyanla and you must welcome this child as an Ajowan. It has been ordained by the creators!"

The lead Spirit Ruler held up a totem that had been painted just that morning and said, "It is already done, dear Prince. You are legally married to Princess Namibia."

Shango looked to Soraya again. She wept quietly and bowed her head so that he could not see her eyes.

"Tonight," Rain Iyanla said to her son, sweetly. "We will have a huge celebration feast. You will undo the virginity of each of your concubines and then you will take to the bed of Namibia as your wife. We will plan a formal wedding, of course, a royal wedding for all the tribes to attend, but..."

"NO!" shouted Shango Ogun, furiously. He dashed off through the crowd and exited through the royal gate. The citizens gasped in disbelief and the soldiers were instructed by Kofi Hoodi to go after Shango and drag him back, but then Mother Iyanla stood up quickly and imitated the sound of a hawk, her old black face commanding, "*Let him go*! My grandson is a young man of high ideals and great passion. He needs time to think this over and I am sure that he will return to us in agreement. This whole miracle has been a shocking event for all of us. We need time to become one with it."

"Got-Baggah, mother!" cursed Kofi Hoodi, furiously. "If he doesn't return, you will bear the blame for it, I may even chop off your head! You have spoiled that boy since the day he was born."

"No, Hoodi," said Mother Iyanla with a solmenly raised chin and hurt feelings. "It was you that I spoiled as a baby. That is why you harbor this greed to take over the world and make senseless war against the God tribe. It is you whose heart...is not a heart, my spoiled rotten son."

"He had better return!" warned Kofi Hoodi as his infuriated gaze burned across his mother's face. He stomped his bare foot and curse-roared again, "*Got-Baggah*!"

••

Shango ran. His heart beating with a wildness, his eyes, hair and skin craving the open sea. But if he went there, they would find him easily, so he went the opposite way.

Into the jungled hills of Batubba. Up them and over them.

He ran and ran until the lack of a planned destination turned the bright moon into an all-seeing glowing pearl that he imagined was chasing him, or *leading* him, he couldn't tell which, to the ends of the earth. He stared at it often, his brow heavy with confusion, his heart pregnant with a passion that only the moon could understand, and eventually, from staring at it so often, the madness and longing in its white glow began to seep beneath the membrane of his mind.

There was something inside him, he realized, that he wanted to bring *out* of him and behold with the naked eye, not the inner one. It was like a thirst, of which languages had no adequate name for, but it kept him running--towards a different kind of sea, a different kind of water.

In trees he slept at night and kept a makeshift torch to ward off any hungry animals that might pick up his scent despite the camphor and ash he kept slathered between the crack of his ass, under his arms and on his feet. From his tree branch he stared at the moon's mysterious glow every night and wondered as lions and apes had wondered--how can I pull it from the sky?

And then, too, he became filled with the moon's loneliness and its obsession with earth. His stare beholding it until he could see that it was not beautiful and magical, but cold and stoney, and even still, Shango could not let it go, its spiritual glare calling him by generations of names.

"*Leave me alone*!" he shouted, leaping from a tree one early morning.

He waded deeper and deeper into the jungle, his eyes suddenly falling upon a group of fifty traveling Sula women--the renegade women and runaways of all the different tribes who lived their lives in protest of the male dominated societies of Africa. The Ajowans called them "*fire witches,*" but they called themselves after the legendary disobedient wife, Sula, a

Fulani woman who had been stoned to death for refusing to allow that her daughters be properly cut (vaginally circumsized) as the men required for marriage.

When Shango ran into them, he had come to a panther's halt, because the Sula women were greatly adept at using the poison-tipped spears they brandished and were known to kill, skin and make carrying bags out of any men they came across, but to his surprise, they only smiled at Shango and gave him a sack cloth full of food and wine. He informed them that he was the Prince of Ajowa, fully expecting them to get in line, kneel and kiss his feet, but they received the news of his royalty as though it were nothing more than old stale wind.

The lead Sula boasted, proudly, "I set my husband on fire and drowned my sons. My daughter and I have never been happier. We have a good life now."

Around her neck hung the shrunken heads of her husband and sons. She took Shango by the hand and led him to a large fallen tree where a herd of giraffes stretched their long necks in the distance. There she sat him down and then motioned for one of the girls to kneel between his legs and suck his penis until it jerked inside her mouth. The girl gave Shango much pleasure and after it was over the Sula women clapped and nodded.

"Now we must go," the Sula leader said while patting Shango on the head. "Enjoy the food we've given you and be very careful on your journeys. Here--take one of our poisoned spears, brother. This will be a good weapon to have."

"Thank you my sisters," intoned Shango as the marching sheen of outlaw women and girls departed into the jungle like a pretty black snake eating yellow fruit and singing, "I don't wish to be a wife...I prefer to *live* my life!"

••

The food they'd given Shango was not the fresh Ajowan seafood he was used to. It was inland food--ground nut paste, antelope meat in a fruit jelly, termites rolled in thin sheets of lizard skin, peppered wheat chips, Fulani rice cakes. Delicious as it all was, it caused a cramp in Shango's belly by nightfall, and just as he was crossing a shallow, narrow waterbed in the Okebo river, he bent over in delirium, his vision blurring and his senses overcharged as though he'd been smoking from the hemp pipe on prayer ritual day.

"I'm high," he said to himself in amazement.

*Then...*a voice whispered in his ear, very gently, "*Shango*".

It frightened the Prince and he dashed out of the riverbed, his knees falling against pebbles as he reached the other side. He heard the voice again, for it said to him--"*look at me,*" and when he looked up at the purple sky...he saw not one, but two moons.

Two full moons, the brightness of which generated a serene, quiet warmth that he had never before felt at nighttime. It was like being underwater. Their white shining beauty more harmonious than birds. The voice of them speaking as one, both male and female, the voice admonishing, "*I am the dolphin girl. I am love...don't let me be lonely.*"

Dolphin girl? Shango's face filled with wonder, because he had seen her as a child, but people had convinced him that he had been hallucinating...imaging things. "You're no better than Beeni and the make believe elves that live under her breasts," they used to say. "There's no such thing as a girl with a dolphin's tail."

But Shango had seen her as a boy. She lived under the sea and had hair just like his--dense and wooly black, thick and knotted. Her color had been truer than his, a cooked chocolate African black, her flat, wide nose reminding Shango of the sensual paint and feather women that danced seductively at the men's fire rituals--why she'd even had their womanish jellyfish shaped mouths--and yet her lower body had been pure silver...whiplashing through the sea, a graceful dolphin's tail and a fin jetting from her back.

"I saw her!" Shango testified, his eyes bulging at the realization that it hadn't been a hallucination, but real...and then he looked back up at the two moons--but now there was only one.

A solitary moon that begged him, "*Please...0 Please...I am very lonely this way. I have nothing but misery and no company to share it with. I am very sad.*"

"Leave me alone...I have no power to please you!" hollered Shango, angrily. He didn't like being talked to by the moon, because it made both butterflies in his stomach and a violent hardness in his loins.

"*Take the poisoned spea,r*" the Moon replied, soothingly. "*...and lick it with your tongue. Don't let me be alone. Lick the spear of death, Shango...just as sweetly as the Sula girl licked the spear of life.*"

Lick it.

Give me your heart. Go into the ground.

Shango knew then that the Moon had nothing at all to do with the dolphin girl--for the Moon was bitter and cold and too ancient and too wise to take pity on anything that lived.

"*Don't let me be lonely...come to me.*"

"No!" shouted Shango, defiantly.

And with that he lifted his powerfully muscular arm...and he vaulted the poisoned spear into the center of the Moon, but of course, anything thrown into the air by humans falls back to earth. So Shango took up running again. His long, sinewy black legs leaping like a cheetah's across the rugged open plains of the mysterious African landscape.

And the Moon said to him: "*I am the Moon...you think you can run from my lonely nights*?"

Shango bolted into the jungle, his feet faster than lightning as he navigated plants, snakes, fallen trees and anything else that stood in his way.

"I am everywhere. Over land and sea and in all the caves and upon the backs of all the birds and all the beasts that sojourn in the dark. I am the teardrop that time forgot. I am the Moon!...and my loneliness...is *everywhere*! I am the separation..."

Shango kept running, his heart beating wildly, his body sucking air, his arms...desperately reaching through jungle for the future.

"...the misery you are born knowing. I am the white diamond that beguiles your vision and inspires *motherless* blue melodies to fall like rotten teeth from your gilded lips."

"I am the eye forever watching the sea...hoping against hope that she will leap from it once more, the dolphin girl for whom time began...to age the wood. I am the eye forever spying...this bitter earth. I am the wreckage of dreams that spin in your heads like doorways to insanity and paradise."

Shango broke open ground again and continued to bolt forward, his body drenched in sweat.

"I am old...and cold...because I am the Moon, and I am alone with my fate...waiting for daybreak."

Every night. Every night. ***Every*** *night.*

I am the Moon.

About the Editor

Mark Fogarty is a New Jersey poet, journalist, musician, editor, and publisher. He has edited and published books under three separate brands: Valley Press, White Chickens Press, and igotmuse.com. His titles include *Inspire the Planet, Went to See the Gypsy, Intimations, Blue Chevies, Rutherford Red Wheelbarrow Poets Anthology, Myshkin's Blues, Christmas Cheer,* and *Equestrienne Dances.*

www.ingramcontent.com/pod-product-compliance
Lightning Source LLC
LaVergne TN
LVHW090947080826
845145LV00003B/915

* 9 7 8 0 5 7 8 0 2 8 9 6 5 *